Falling into Place

Stephanie Greene

CLARION BOOKS
New York

Clarion Books
a Houghton Mifflin Company imprint
215 Park Avenue South, New York, NY 10003
Copyright © 2002 by Stephanie Greene
First Clarion paperback edition, 2006.

The text was set in 12-point Stempel Garamond.

www.houghtonmifflinbooks.com

Printed in the U.S.A.

Library of Congress Cataloging-in-Publication Data

Greene, Stephanie.
Falling into place / Stephanie Greene.
p. cm.
Summary: As eleven-year-old Margaret struggles to find a way of coping with
the hassles of a new stepfamily, she learns that her Gran is facing similar
concerns after moving to a retirement community and becoming a widow.
ISBN: 0-618-17744-2
[1. Grandmothers—Fiction. 2. Stepfamilies—Fiction. 3. Family life—Fiction.
4. Moving, Household—Fiction.] I. Title.
PZ7.G8434 Fal 2002
[Fic]—dc21   2002002744

CL ISBN–13: 978-0-618-17744-8   CL ISBN–10: 0-618-17744-2
PA ISBN–13: 978-0-618-68928-6   PA ISBN–10: 0-618-68928-1

VB 10 9 8 7 6 5 4 3 2 1

To my brothers and sisters

Before

"Would you like to buy some magic dirt?" asked Margaret.

"Magic dirt?" Gran looked surprised. "Why, that's just what I was looking for. How much is it?"

"It usually costs ten dollars a bag, but today you can buy six bags for a dollar."

"What a bargain! What makes it magic?"

"It makes worms come to your garden."

"That's all fine and well," said Gran, frowning, "but does it cure chicken pox?"

"Noooo."

"What about stomachaches? Does it do anything for those?"

"*Gran!* You're not supposed to *eat* it!"

"Sounds like you two are up to your old tricks

again." Tad came out onto the front porch and rested his fishing pole against the railing.

"Margaret says her magic dirt attracts worms, but it doesn't do a thing about chicken pox," said Gran indignantly.

"As long as the worms like it, I'll take some," said Tad. He pulled a dollar bill from his pocket and held it out to Margaret.

"You get five more bags for that much," she said, picking up one of the brown paper bags in front of her.

"Put 'em on my account." Tad sat down on the top step and opened his tackle box. "Come on, sport. Are we going fishing or aren't we?"

"The picnic's all ready," said Gran. "It won't take more than a minute to mix the lemonade." She disappeared inside the cool, dark front hall.

Margaret sat down next to her grandfather and rested her chin on her hands. In silence she watched him untangling his lures. Then she said, "Tad?"

"Hmm?"

Margaret frowned. "Is Dad going to marry that lady?"

Tad gave her a quick glance. "You mean, Wendy?"

She nodded.

Tad lifted up the top layer of hooks and took

out a pair of clippers. "Well, I can't say for sure, Margaret. Why? You think it's a good idea?"

She shook her head.

"I thought you two seemed to be getting along real well those times she came down here with you and your dad."

"I don't really like her."

"You don't, huh?" Tad took his time unwinding a length of line from the spool, measuring it to the right length, and cutting it. "Your dad says she's a great mother."

"I don't need a mother," Margaret said. "I have Dad."

"Well, it's true that you two have done fine on your own all these years. I guess you don't miss your mom, seeing as she died so soon after you were born." Tad fed the line through the hole in the lure and tied it. Then he put it back in the box and picked up another one. "But mothers can do a lot of things fathers can't," he said. "And what about those little girls? Your dad says they're crazy about you."

"They're babies."

Tad laughed. "Seems to me that's the way you started out, and you didn't turn out so bad," he said, nudging her with his elbow. "Might be nice having three younger sisters to boss around. You can make them clean your room, and do your homework, and stuff."

"I like it just Dad and me," Margaret said stubbornly.

She heard Gran's quick steps coming back down the hall toward them. Gran always moved quickly, whether she was working in the garden or hanging out the wash. She did everything with brisk, efficient motions, like a bird. The screen door burst open, and she came bustling out onto the porch behind them. "I told you it wouldn't take long." Gran put the picnic basket down and looked at them expectantly. "Are you two ready?"

Tad looked up at her over Margaret's head. "We've been talking about Matt and Wendy," he told her. "Margaret's worried they might be planning on getting married."

"Oh, but lovey." Gran sank down on the other side of Margaret and put her arm around her shoulders. "Think of what fun it would be if they did. Wendy's a lovely woman, who loves you and your father very much. You'd have the little girls to play with and share things with. . . . Think of what a big, happy family you'd have."

"We already have a happy family," Margaret said, not looking at her.

"Of course we do." Gran gave her shoulders a

little shake. "And if your father and Wendy get married, it will just be a bit bigger."

"Margaret says she likes it just her and Matt," said Tad.

"Yes . . . Well, there are a lot worse things than having to share someone you love," Gran said firmly. She took her arm from around Margaret and straightened up with resolve. "Besides, there's nothing you or Tad or I can do about it. And don't you worry. No matter what happens, Tad and I will be here to help hold you up. Won't we, Tad?"

"Like bookends," he said cheerfully.

It felt good being sandwiched between the two of them—Gran so small and quick on one side, Tad so tall and calm on the other. Margaret knew they would be there to help her, because they'd *always* been there. But she didn't care what Gran said about there being worse things than sharing someone you loved. She couldn't imagine anything worse than having to share her dad.

"You can't be bookends," she said sourly. "You're uneven."

Gran and Tad laughed. Then Gran said to Tad, "This is all your fault, you know."

"My fault?"

"Look at her." They both leaned in from either side and peered into Margaret's face. She frowned even harder and stared straight ahead, as if there was something very important out in the yard she had to keep her eyes on.

"She doesn't get those frown lines from *my* side of the family," said Gran.

"Hmm, I guess you're right." The tip of Tad's nose was so close, it was almost touching Margaret's cheek. It was all she could do not to reach up and scratch. "My great-aunt Lucy used to grow corn in her furrows," he said. "Looks like Margaret could give her a bit of competition. But what about this?" She tried not to squirm as he ran his finger firmly down her spine, but she couldn't help it. "This is a Hanson stubborn streak if I've ever seen one."

She knew they were trying to make her laugh, but she was determined not to. Then they started to lean against her on either side, gently at first, and then harder, until her shoulders were pressed firmly up against her ears, and her stomach felt like it was going to pop.

It was impossible.

"Hey! You're shmushing me!" she yelped.

When Gran and Tad stopped leaning, Margaret sagged gratefully against Gran's side.

"That's better," said Gran. She patted Margaret's knee and stood up. "Brooding is a waste of time unless you're a hen. Now, come on, we've got work to do." She picked up the two plastic containers she'd left on the rocking chair and handed one to Margaret. "If we're going to have those blueberry pancakes you asked for tomorrow morning, we'd better get picking."

"We might have to eat right here on the porch," said Tad. He glanced up at the sky. "Looks to me like rain."

"On Margaret's last day? It wouldn't dare." Gran started down the steps. "I think you'll have to bring the basket, Tad. Margaret's too small."

"I am not," said Margaret indignantly. She jumped down and stood next to Gran on the walk, standing as straight as she could. "I'm almost as tall as you are, Gran."

"Yes, well, you can be thankful you inherited *that* Mack gene," Gran said. "None of the women in my family have been over five foot two."

"Your grandmother's the tallest of the lot," Tad agreed, "and she's no bigger than a minute."

"Lucky for you I'm not, David Mack," said Gran.

Tad gave a snort of appreciation.

"I think you'd better let Tad take it, Margaret," Gran said to Margaret as she started to cut across the front yard. "It's very heavy."

"Not to me it's not."

"Are you sure?"

"I'm sure." But it *was* heavy. Margaret had to use both hands to lift it up and hold it against her chest. "You must have a lot of food in here," she said.

"All your favorites," called Gran airily. She stopped when she got to the huge maple tree near the end of the walk and put her hand absentmindedly on the rope ladder that hung down from the tree fort. "Tad's Folly" Gran had named it. Anything Margaret asked for, Tad added to it. In addition to the rope ladder it had a swing, a slide that spiraled down to the ground, a bucket on a pulley for Margaret to lift things up in, and a real picture window. Tad was going to build a turret with windows next.

"Are you sure you can manage?" Gran said now.

"Yep."

Too late Margaret recognized the mischievous grin on her grandmother's face.

"Good . . . Then the last one to fill her bowl cleans the breakfast dishes," Gran said, and took off running.

"Hey! No fair!" shouted Margaret. She tried to run, but the basket banged against her legs.

"Looks like she pulled a fast one on you," said Tad. "I'll bring the basket, Margaret. You go get her."

She put it down and ran, but Gran was way

ahead. Margaret didn't catch up to her until Gran was halfway across the field.

Then they walked, hand-in-hand and breathless, the rest of the way to the pond.

Chapter 1.

"Anyone have a hug for a tired man?"

Margaret looked up from her book to see the big, comforting shape of her father framed in the doorway to the family room.

"Dad!" She started up off the couch to go to him, but the little girls were quicker.

"Dad! Daddy! Daddy!" Emily, Sarah, and Claire scrambled across the room and hurled themselves at Mr. Mack like puppies looking for a treat. He laughed and pretended to stagger back from the weight of them as the twins wrapped their skinny arms around his legs and Claire grabbed him around his waist and pressed her face into his jacket.

"Matt! What a wonderful surprise," Wendy said, coming out of the kitchen. She leaned in toward him over the girls' heads for a kiss. "You weren't supposed to get home until tonight."

"I took the redeye," said Mr. Mack. He looked at her worriedly. "You sounded tired on the phone last night."

"Oh, it's just that it's been so hot." Wendy pushed her damp curly blond hair back off her forehead and rested her hands on top of her huge stomach as if it was a shelf. "I have to admit, I'm glad you're home."

Watching them, Margaret started to get her funny balloon feeling again. The one she'd gotten for the first time almost a year ago, right after Dad and Wendy got married and the little girls had surrounded him with their curly blond hair and huge blue eyes so much like Wendy's and called him "Dad" over and over again, just for the sound of it. It had given Margaret the strangest feeling, as if she was a balloon a child had let go of, and she was floating up into the sky, higher and higher, with nothing to hold her down, until, before anyone knew it, she would be a faint speck in the white part of the sky, alone. . . .

"Whoa! Hold on for a minute!" Mr. Mack held up his hands. "We need to do a head count. One, two, three . . ." He put his hand first on Sarah's head, then Emily's, then Claire's. "I thought so. We're missing one." He looked up with an expectant smile toward the couch. "Where's Mar—?"

Margaret shut her bedroom door, sat down on her bed, and pushed herself back until she was resting against the wall. She crossed her arms tightly over her chest.

It was all right. She didn't need to hug her dad the minute he came home from a trip. That was what she used to do when she was little. Maybe babies needed a hug when their dad had been gone for a week. But not eleven-year-olds.

Anyway, it wasn't as if Dad missed *her* hugs. Why should he? He got so many of them now. Not once, in all the months since Wendy and the girls had come to live with them, had he ever said, "Where's my number-one hugger?" the way he used to. Maybe he'd gotten tired of having only one person around to hug, she thought. Maybe he liked being hugged by three little girls who were so much younger and prettier than she was.

She got up and went over to her dresser and stared hard at her face in the mirror. Horrible brown hair, dark heavy eyebrows over plain brown eyes. Nose too thin, mouth too wide. She frowned, and watched with grim satisfaction as the furrows between her eyes deepened. When she heard a soft knock at the door, she whirled around. The door opened a crack. Claire stuck her head around the edge and looked at Margaret with huge eyes.

"Margaret," she said breathlessly, "Daddy brought us presents! Come see."

Claire looked like an angel. Everybody said so. She had a mass of curly blond hair and dark blue eyes, and a neck so delicate it looked as if her head could topple right off.

An angel who clung to Dad every time he came into the room, Margaret thought, watching her. An angel who seemed to appear from nowhere whenever Margaret got her father to herself, and squeeze in between them so insistently it made Mr. Mack laugh.

Margaret felt a sudden urge to wipe the happy, excited look off Claire's face. "He's not really *your* daddy," she said slowly. "He's mine."

Claire's mouth fell open and then froze in an astonished "O." She blinked once as tears rose in her eyes like water up the side of a glass. And then as suddenly as she had arrived, she disappeared, and the door closed with a soft click.

Margaret walked back over to her bed and sat down. She shouldn't have said that. She hadn't really meant to hurt Claire. It was just so hard sometimes, this new life of hers. Dad and Wendy kept talking about how great it was that she was eleven going on twelve. How mature she was, compared to the little girls. But she didn't feel mature. Sometimes, like now, when she could feel a lump rising in her throat, she felt like a baby.

There was another knock at the door. This time it was her dad.

"Hi." He hesitated with his hand on the door-knob. "Can I come in?"

"I guess."

Mr. Mack shut the door behind him and came over and sat down on the edge of her bed next to her. He rested his warm hand on her knee. "You disappeared so quickly, I didn't get to say hello." He smiled a questioning smile. "You're getting too old for hugs, is that it?"

"Kind of." Margaret looked down at her lap, hiding her face from him with a curtain of hair.

"Did you miss me?" he said.

She shrugged.

"*I* missed *you*." He waited. When she didn't reply, he reached out and tucked a strand of her hair behind her ear. "It sounds like it was kind of a tough week," he said.

"It was okay."

She could feel her dad looking at her. "Wendy told me about the game you made up for the girls in the basement," he said at last. "She's afraid she may have overreacted."

Margaret looked up into his dark brown eyes that

were so much like her own. "I *told* Claire the queen was going to be arrested and thrown in the dungeon," she said fiercely. "Dungeons *have* to be dark. I *said* we had to tie the queen up so she wouldn't escape. I said *I* would be the queen. But Claire always has to be the queen, or she cries."

"Wendy knows that," said her dad. "It's just that Claire's afraid of the dark, and Wendy was worried your game was going to make it worse."

"Claire's afraid of everything," said Margaret. She looked down into her lap again quickly. The sympathy in his voice wasn't for her, it was for Claire.

"Hey, come on." His voice was gentle. "This hasn't been an easy summer for any of us, Margaret. It's so hot, everyone's cranky. Wendy says the little girls have been wild all week. After the baby's born, we'll go to the shore for a week. Things will get back to normal."

Oh, no, they won't, thought Margaret dully. Things were never going to get back to normal. Normal had disappeared the day she ran out to the car after school in the third grade and found a woman she'd never seen before sitting in the front seat next to her dad. *Margaret's* seat, which had been hers for her whole life, practically. All Dad had said was, "Margaret, this is Wendy. Hop in the back, like a good girl."

After that, everything that was normal in her life had started to fall. Like dominoes when they're set up on one end and spaced the perfect distance apart, so that when the first one is pushed, the rest follow in a constant ripple until the last one is knocked over.

First, Wendy came to dinner with "three surprises"—Claire, Emily, and Sarah.

Then Gran called to say Tad was sick.

Then Wendy and Dad got married.

Then Gran and Tad had to sell the house on Blackberry Lane and move to Carol Woods so nurses could take care of Tad.

Then Dad said Wendy was having a baby.

Then Tad died.

Plinkplinkplinkplinkplinkplink.

Margaret had thought all the dominoes in her life that could be knocked over had been. Until yesterday. Yesterday, when Wendy called to her from upstairs, and Margaret went running up to find her standing in the doorway to Margaret's room with her arms outstretched and a smile on her face, saying, "What do you think? Isn't it beautiful?"

And there was Claire's bed, pushed up against the wall where Margaret's desk had been, and a pink rug on the floor. All night long, she'd had to listen to loud crinkling noises every time Claire turned over.

She was sharing her room with a six-year-old bed wetter, and Dad hadn't even talked to her about it first.

"Come on." The weight of his hand on her head made her look up. For the first time, she saw that his face was drawn and tired, and that the nerve under his right eye that twitched when he was getting a headache was pulsing rhythmically. "Is it really as bad as all that?" he said.

The answer was on the tip of her tongue, but she didn't say it. He didn't really want to know. They had had this discussion a million times. He wanted her to be on his side. He wanted her to cope. To grow up, and act eleven. Even if the only difference between being ten and being eleven was one tiny second.

When the screen door under her bedroom window slammed, they both started. There was the sound of running footsteps, then wheels spinning furiously on the gravel driveway.

A shrill tricycle bell rang.

"I'm sick of them," Margaret said. "Everything they wear is pink. Their shoes are pink, their pajamas are pink, even their underwear is pink. I'm sick of it."

"Pink?" He sat back, amazed. "That's what this is all about? The color pink?" He laughed a kind of giddy, relieved laugh. "Would it make you feel any better if I made them wear brown?"

"It's not funny, Dad."

He was immediately somber again. "I know it's not. Listen." He clamped his hand around her knee and held it there, as if steadying a nervous colt. "You know what I think? I think you need a break. How would you like to go to Gran's?"

Gran. The moment Margaret heard the word, a feeling of relief surged up in her so strong that she rose onto her knees without realizing she had moved. "Could I, Dad? Could I really? By myself?"

"She called last week to invite you, but I told her I thought you wanted to be here when the baby was born."

"Oh, I don't care. . . . I mean, I do care, I do." She backtracked quickly to wipe away the hurt look on his face. "It's just that I haven't stayed with Gran since Tad died. I miss her so much. You don't need me around here. Wendy's had lots of babies without my help."

"We weren't exactly expecting you to deliver it," said her father.

"Oh, I know. I didn't mean it that way." Margaret clasped her hands together and willed herself to slow down. He *had* to say yes. If he didn't let her go to Gran's, she would die.

"Gran needs me," she said carefully. "You said you thought she was lonely. She wouldn't be if I was there. She's never lonely with me around. I could help her dig a garden, and we could take long walks, and watch old movies. . . . Oh, please, Dad?"

He looked at her for what felt like a very long time. His expression was serious, as if he was looking for a way to tell her no so she wouldn't be disappointed. And then his face changed, and she knew he had made up his mind.

"Okay." He smiled. "I'll go call her now."

"Oh, thank you, thank you!" Margaret cried. She leapt up off her bed and started to twirl deliriously around the room. Gran! Someone to talk to. Someone who would understand. She would tell Gran everything. About the dominoes, about Claire, about Dad . . . Margaret crashed into her dresser and yanked open the top drawer, pulling out socks and underwear like a thief ransacking a house.

Her dad watched her from the doorway with an amused expression on his face. "We'll call you the minute the baby's born," he said.

"Not if it's after nine o'clock—you know Gran." Margaret flopped down on her stomach and felt around under her bed for her shoes. "Can I take the train like I did when I was nine?" she said with her cheek pressed against the rug. When her hand settled on the familiar shape of her sneaker, she pulled it out and sat up. "I remember everything," she recited. "I get off at Chester—it's the eighth stop. My grand-parents are Mr. and Mrs. David Mack. Well, it's only Mrs. Mack now. Their telephone number is 555—" She stopped. "Does Gran have the same number?"

"Yep."

"Good. Then it's 555-9244. See?"

"I'm impressed," said her dad. "It's been a while."

"Almost two years," said Margaret. Her first train trip alone to stay with her grandparents had been their ninth birthday present to her. It was only a short ride, but she could still remember how it felt sitting next to the huge window on the slippery leather seat, gently rocking from side to side as the train raced down the tracks. The backs of houses and stores and factories rushed by, and the air was filled with the faint smell of metal. She'd had a flutter in her stomach every time the train slowed down to pull into a station, wondering if it was her stop. What if she got off too early? Or what if she realized it was the right one only as the train was pulling out?

The minute the train pulled into Chester, she had relaxed. There was no mistaking it. Gran and Tad were standing on the platform with a white sign that said MISS MACK in huge red letters, like limousine drivers waiting for someone important. They had promised they would meet her that way every year.

Even though Tad was gone, Margaret knew Gran would remember.

She could hardly wait.

She opened her closet door to look for her suitcase.

"Don't get your hopes too high," her dad cautioned. "Gran doesn't seem to be fitting into Carol Woods the way we hoped. I think Tad's dying so soon after they got there was very hard on her. She doesn't seem to have made any friends. The rules and regulations are getting her down a bit, too. She sounded kind of flat the last time I talked to her."

"Gran doesn't care about rules," said Margaret.

"I'm afraid that when you live in a retirement community, you have to."

"Not Gran."

"Just don't get her all worked up over them, all right?"

"Don't worry." Margaret spotted the orange handle of her suitcase under a pile of junk at the bottom of her closet and knelt down. "I'll cheer her up. Gran's always happy when I'm around."

Her dad didn't say anything for a minute. Then, "What about that hug?"

Margaret paused with her hand on the handle. She knew that she should get up and run across the room and throw her arms around his waist, that she wouldn't get to hug him again until she got back from Gran's. But for the first time in her life, she didn't feel like it. Anyway, he'd have plenty of hugs while she was gone.

And she'd have Gran.

There was a sudden wail from outside, followed by a second, angrier, wail. Margaret yanked at the handle and fell back against her bed as the suitcase shot out onto her lap.

"Emily probably took Sarah's bike," she said without turning around. "You'd better get out there. Remember what happened the last time?"

"Oh, great, and Wendy's taking a nap." Her dad was halfway down the stairs by the time Margaret stood up and laid her suitcase on her bed. She heard the back door slam, then his deep voice from outside.

Plink.

It didn't feel good, having another domino fall. But at least this time she'd been the one who'd done the pushing.

Chapter 2.

"Oh, stop sniveling," said Margaret. "It's just a little blood and gravel."

"I'm not sniveling. My nose is running and I have to breathe it back in." Roy cupped his hand around the bloody patch that was his knee. "I think I can see bone."

"You should have taken a running jump, like I told you." Margaret licked at the trail of cherry Popsicle that was running from her wrist to her elbow. She stared down at him from the top of the stone wall.

She still couldn't get over the shock she'd felt yesterday when she saw Roy as the train pulled into the station. There was Gran, standing where Margaret had known she would be. Margaret's heart had started to soar, but then, just as quickly, it had stopped. Gran wasn't alone. A little boy with round tortoiseshell glasses and an expectant look on his face was standing next to her. Her cousin Roy, who wasn't even supposed to *be* there. The way his hand was tucked so comfortably into Gran's as he leaned against her had given Margaret the strangest feeling. As if she was the visitor and he was the one who belonged there.

Margaret was so surprised, it had taken her a few minutes to notice the change in Gran. She seemed frail, somehow, not just small, and anxious. She gave Margaret a hurried hug instead of her usual warm embrace, and then grabbed Margaret's hand. "Sign? What sign? Hold on to my hand, Margaret." Her voice was loud and querulous. "Roy, where are you? Stay close to me now, both of you."

She clutched Margaret to her on one side and Roy on the other as she pulled them down the platform. The way she kept them clutched so insistently to her side, it was as if there was a huge crowd on the platform and she was afraid they were going to be swept onto the tracks. But there wasn't any crowd. Other than the two people hurrying to their cars at the other end of the platform, they were the only people there.

It wasn't like Gran at all to be so nervous. And it had given Margaret a fluttery feeling in the pit of her stomach. How could she talk to Gran about *her* problems when Gran seemed so worried herself? And even if Gran was all right, how was she ever going to get her to herself?

She would never forgive Roy if he ruined her visit with Gran. Never.

Not only was he almost as big a baby as Claire, but he was uncoordinated. He couldn't play the simplest game of follow-the-leader without hurting himself. Claire followed orders much better than he did, too. When Margaret told him to close his eyes and take a running jump to get over the gap in the stone wall where the walkway ran through, he refused. And now look at him, she thought disgustedly. Another baby, crying.

She jumped down off the wall and walked over to where he sat huddled on the grass. "I never cry," she said, taking another lick of her Popsicle. "I didn't even cry when I broke my collarbone, and that hurt a lot more than your dumb old knee."

"How do you know?" said Roy. He squeezed his wound gently. "See that white thing?"

"That's just the inside of your skin," said Margaret. She made a disgusted clicking noise. "You're a bigger baby than Claire."

"It stings like crazy."

"Oh, for Pete's sake, hold still." She squatted down next to him, grabbed his knee, and started rubbing the tip of her Popsicle back and forth vigorously over his wound.

"Keep it down, would you?" she said, ducking to avoid his flailing arms. "You make it sound like you're being murdered. Hey!" Margaret jumped to her feet and rubbed the side of her head where he'd struck her. "What'd you do that for?"

"You can't put Popsicle on an open wound!" Roy's round face was screwed up into a furious knot. "It's full of sugar!"

"So? Look at that—a perfectly good Popsicle, wasted," she said disgustedly. See if she ever tried to help *him* out again! She broke off the top, tossed it back over her shoulder, and put what was left of it back in her mouth. "You could have given me a concussion," she said.

"That's better than gangrene," said Roy. He pushed himself up off the ground with his injured leg held stiffly out in front of him, and started moving along the wall with jerky, birdlike hops.

Margaret followed along behind him, swinging a stiff leg out to the side in an exaggerated arc, and moaning.

"It's not funny, Margaret," said Roy. He hobbled faster to put a greater distance between them, and stopped. Like a swimmer testing the water with a fearful toe, he rested his foot on the ground and put his full weight on it. As she came up to him, Margaret heard the sharp intake of his breath.

"It feels better, doesn't it?" she said.

"No."

"Yes, it does, I can tell. Go on, try walking."

"I don't know what you're in such a bad mood about," Roy said to her. "But you'd better stop being mean to me, Margaret, or I'm telling Gran."

Margaret felt a moment of panic. If Roy went running back to Gran, upset, she didn't know *what* Gran would do. Not after the way she had acted last night, when all Roy did was call the stew she put in front of them "Tad's favorite." Without warning, Gran's mouth had gone slack and her eyes had gotten a bewildered, lost look. She'd said something vague about having to get the salad, and then turned and made her way back into the kitchen, holding on to the backs of the chairs as if she needed to be shown the way. Margaret and Roy had sat there in shocked silence.

When Gran finally came back into the room, she acted as if nothing had happened. But Margaret couldn't forget the look on her face. She couldn't bear to think of Gran looking that way again.

"We were sent to try and cheer her up, remember?" she said, in a voice far more confident than she felt. "How do you think she's going to feel, knowing her grandson's a tattletale?"

"Then you better stop telling me what to do," said Roy.

"Okay, okay." Margaret bit off the last piece of her Popsicle and held the stick up in front of her face. "Want to hear a joke?"

"What?"

"What gets colder as it warms up?"

"I don't know," said Roy. He started to limp again.

"An air conditioner." She stuck the stick behind one ear and fell in next to him.

"What'd you do that for?" Roy said.

"I'm thinking about making a Popsicle-stick joke book. If I don't save the sticks, I'll forget the jokes."

"Your ear's going to get infected, putting that thing back there."

"All you do is talk about things getting infected all the time," Margaret said, glad to be on a safer topic.

"I can't help it. My father's a doctor."

They walked slowly, moving in and out of the shadows of the trees that fell across the road in stripes. There was a row of small white cottages on either side of the street. Each one had a small front yard hemmed in by a picket fence. The shutters and doors were black.

Gran didn't like the houses at Carol Woods, Margaret could tell. She said she got lost every time she went out, they all looked so much alike. But they didn't, really. Each one had something different about it if you looked carefully. The one Margaret and Roy were passing had bright red geraniums in green window boxes on the front. The one next to it had sunflowers that reached to the top of the door.

Margaret thought they were pretty. She thought Carol Woods looked like a little village, and the houses reminded her of the cozy houses in picture books, where neighbors leaned over their picket fences and borrowed a cup of sugar. It would be nice to have neighbors so close in the middle of a thunderstorm, she thought, especially if you were alone. But when she had said this to Gran on the way home from the station yesterday, Gran had said she didn't know any of her neighbors yet and wasn't sure she wanted to.

"All anyone talks about in a place like this is their aches and pains and what medicines they take." Gran's voice was full of scorn. "It doesn't make for very interesting conversation."

Margaret had frowned. It wasn't like Gran to be so mean. Especially about people she didn't even know. She was always telling Margaret not to judge people before she got to know them. And on Blackberry Lane Gran had been friends with all the neighbors.

"How do you know if you don't even know them?" Margaret had said insistently. But Gran didn't answer.

That wasn't like her, either.

Margaret gave a nervous little side hop as if trying to get away from herself. Here she was, thinking about Gran again. She whirled around to face Roy. "Want to get some sheets and build a fort when we get back?"

"Maybe. But you can't make all the rules from now on," he said. "You're only twenty-eight months older than me. You're not the boss of me. We both are. Gran said so."

"But I have more experience than you," said Margaret. "I boss the girls around all the time. You don't have anyone to boss."

"Girls are different. Boys don't like being bossed."

"Neither do girls," she said breezily, and then threw her hands over her head, hopped up on one foot, and kicked over slowly from a handstand into a back bend. "The thing about bossing is," she said, with her dark hair falling to the ground like a beard, "you're not supposed to ask the person whether they like it or not."

Roy stared at her disapprovingly. "You're going to hurt your backbone, staying like that," he said. "You could get curvature of the spine."

"Go on," she grunted. "Time me."

He pressed a button on his watch and kept his eye on it until Margaret let out a burst of air and collapsed onto the grass with her legs doubled back beneath her. "Fifty-six seconds," he said.

"You didn't start on time." She pulled a strand of hair out of the corner of her mouth and jumped to her feet. "I usually go longer than that."

They started walking again.

"*I* was sent to cheer her up," said Roy, picking up where they left off. "*You* were sent because they were trying to get rid of you."

"Rid of me?" Margaret stopped. "You don't know what you're talking about."

"I do, too. I heard Gran talking to him on the phone before you came. Your dad said you were being a handful and Gran said that must make it hard on everyone. Then she said, 'Why don't you send Margaret here?'"

There was a hollow feeling in the pit of her stomach. She should have known. Dad had made it sound as if he was trying to be nice to *her*. But that wasn't it at all. All he really cared about was Wendy and the girls. They were probably having a much better time at home without her, sitting together in the family room with the twins on the floor in their usual tangled heap and Claire on the couch between Wendy and Dad, peacefully enjoying being a family. Without her.

"A handful of what?" she said, tossing her hair back over her shoulder as if she didn't care.

"Not a handful *of* anything," said Roy. He pulled a small notebook out of his back pocket and opened it. "It means you're hard to handle. I looked it up. The first definition is 'A small amount or quantity,' but that's not what Uncle Matt meant." He stopped and ran his finger down a page. "He meant, 'Someone or something that is as much as one can handle.' As in," here he looked at Margaret with the sun glinting off his glasses, "'That child is a real handful.'"

"As in?" said Margaret. She was suddenly wildly, amazingly angry. At Roy . . . at Dad . . . at herself. She didn't know where to direct her anger, it was so new and blazing hot.

"Do you know what a nerd you are, writing down words like that?" she said. Her wide mouth flattened into a disapproving line. "Everyone at school must make fun of you."

"I don't mind." Roy looked back at her with a friendly, unguarded expression on his face. "Words are interesting."

As hard as she tried to stare him down, he didn't

flinch. "I can't believe this," she said finally. She turned on her heel and started to walk as quickly as she could. A slight breeze ruffled the leaves overhead, and the faint sound of a lawn mower started up somewhere in the distance. Walking in and out of the shadows of the trees had a regular, calming effect, Margaret thought, like a metronome. She could hear Roy trotting along in companionable silence behind her.

"I don't think being a handful's so bad," he piped up suddenly. "It must be pretty interesting sometimes."

She stopped and looked at him in amazement. He was trying to be kind. She had just insulted him and had marched off in a huff trying to ignore him, and here he was, being nice to her. Her anger went up in a puff of smoke.

"Remember when you came to our house last summer?" she said to him.

"That was fun."

"Remember when I told you I hated you, and you cried?" She shook her head. "That was so amazing."

"I don't think it was amazing," Roy said. "You hurt my feelings."

"But I say that to the girls all the time, and they say it to me," said Margaret. "It doesn't really mean anything."

"To me it does."

"No one says it to you because you're an only child," she said, remembering.

"They don't that much. All I have is my parents." Roy thought for a minute. "Do your *parents* tell you they hate you?"

"Of course not," said Margaret. It was true. As many times as she might have thought about hating Wendy, Wendy had never once thought about hating her, she suddenly realized. She didn't know how she knew it, but she did. And it made her feel so glad, she laughed.

"Come on." She stepped up onto the edge of the curb and held her arms out to the sides. "Both arms out and no looking at your feet," she said.

"Okay," said Roy, stepping up behind her. "But no more stone walls."

"Okay."

"What do you think the baby will be?" said Roy after a while.

"Are you joking? All Wendy has is girls."

"Maybe having another girl will be nice," he said. "It was kind of fun, having them around. When they weren't crying, that is."

"Which is never." Margaret started to hop on one foot. "That's easy for you to say. You don't have to listen to Sarah making snurgling noises through the wall every night."

"Snurgling?" Roy sounded interested. "I don't think that's a word."

"It should be."

"What does snurgling sound like?"

Margaret stopped. "Kind of like little bubbles are coming out of your nose, and you're breathing through your mouth with phlegm in the back of your throat." She started up again, on the other foot this time. "Sarah won't wear anything except her bathing suit, so she always has a cold."

"Even in winter?" said Roy. He fell off the curb for the second time and gave up, following along behind her in the road.

"That's better than Emily," Margaret said. "For a long time, she wouldn't wear anything at all."

"*Nothing?*"

"Except boots. You couldn't turn your back on her for a minute." Margaret leapt off the curb and spun around. "No fair, cheater!"

But there wasn't any passion in it. They were home.

Margaret felt a strange sinking feeling as she looked at Gran's front door. It was black, like all the other doors. When they'd first moved into Carol Woods, Gran said she was going to paint it a different color every spring, the way she'd painted the front door at Blackberry Lane different colors. But then she found out that there was a rule against it, so she didn't. Looking at it now, Margaret wished it was yellow or red—any color other than black that would mean Gran was behind it, the old Gran, the happy Gran.

"What's wrong?" said Roy.

Margaret looked at him, startled. She'd forgotten for a moment that he was there. "Why should anything be wrong?"

"You look kind of funny."

"Look who's talking." She peered at him closely for the first time. "You're a mess," she said, poking her finger into the hem of her T-shirt to make a washcloth.

"No spit," he said, pulling back.

"No spit." She put her hand on the back of his neck, the way she'd learned to do with the girls, and scrubbed at his face until the tear tracks running out from under his glasses joined with a dirty circle around his mouth. "There," she said. "That's better."

Margaret opened the gate and started toward the house.

"We'd better be quiet," Roy whispered. "She might be taking a nap."

"Who, Gran?" The thought horrified her. "Gran doesn't take naps."

"She did the day before you got here. She fell

asleep in her chair, sitting up. . . ." His voice trailed off.

"That's ridiculous," Margaret snapped. "Only babies take naps."

She grabbed the knocker and rapped it against the door like a fireman come to alert the house to the fact that flames were shooting out of an upstairs window. "Gran!" she cried, throwing open the front door. "We're back!"

And there was Gran, coming in through the doors from the back patio with a smile on her face and a trowel in her hand, awake.

Chapter 3.

"There you are!" said Gran. She sounded surprised and pleased, as if they had all been playing hide-and-seek and she had been scouring the house for them, checking under beds and behind doors. Until at last she'd found them crouched behind a pile of clothing in the closet, giggling.

"Roy said you were taking a nap, but I knew you weren't," said Margaret. She ran across the room and threw her arms around Gran's waist.

"Margaret, you'll cut me in two!" Gran protested, laughing.

Margaret let go and stood back. "You were gardening," she said with satisfaction. Gran looked happy. She had a smudge of dirt on one cheek, the knees of her jeans were stained green, and her big toe was poking its way through a hole in her sneaker. It was the way Gran had looked at Blackberry Lane. She always seemed to be either going out to the garden behind the house, or coming in from it. That garden was huge. Sometimes Margaret helped her weed. Other times, they sat together and ate ripe tomatoes right off the vine with the juice running down their arms to their elbows.

Margaret fell into a large, soft chair next to the fireplace. "Are you going to grow strawberries and squash, like you used to?" she said happily.

"With the space I have?" Gran put the trowel on the table and started to peel off her gardening gloves. "I'm afraid not. I'll be lucky if I can coax a few tomatoes into life in pots. I only get about two hours of sun on the terrace."

"Why don't you make a compost pile?" said Roy, lying comfortably on his stomach on the rug. "That would help."

"It's not allowed."

"Says who?" said Margaret.

"Mr. Roland Whiting," said Gran crisply.

"Who's he?"

"President of the Carol Woods Steering Committee." Gran sat down on the couch and tucked a piece of hair back into the bun at the nape of her neck. Her face, which was usually so tan, was pale. "No compost piles . . . no clotheslines . . . no color . . ." Her face grew still. "No signs of humanity of any kind."

There was a heavy silence in the room. Watching Gran, Margaret was suddenly reminded of a conversation she'd overheard between Dad and Wendy in the living room one night. The little girls were asleep and she was supposed to be reading in bed, but she'd tiptoed down the hall to crouch in her usual hiding spot behind the banister in the upstairs hall.

"Mom got another letter from Mr. Whiting," her dad said.

"What is he objecting to this time?"

Her dad sighed. "Remember the flowered curtains that used to be in Margaret's room at Blackberry Lane? Mom hung them in her new guest room as a surprise."

"Oh, Matt." Wendy sounded sympathetic. "What's wrong with that?"

"Nothing, you would think, but Carol Woods has an exterior appearance rule, and Mom broke it."

"And what is an exterior appearance rule?"

"The residents are allowed to hang only white curtains in their windows," her dad said. "They want all the houses to look the same from the outside."

"Boy, your mother must hate that."

"She does, but Carol Woods is a retirement community, and retirement communities have rules."

"I know they do," Wendy said, "but you have to admit, some of them are pretty silly. Your poor mother had a fit when she got the letter about hanging her wash on the line."

"Rules are rules, Wendy." Her dad's voice had been tired. Margaret could tell he didn't want to talk about it anymore. As she ran back to her bed and slipped beneath the covers, she'd been filled with indignation. Gran will *never* put up with people telling her what to do, she thought as she pulled the blanket up to her chin.

But Gran was putting up with it now.

Margaret sat up. "Why don't you go *talk* to the Steering Committee about it?" she said encouragingly. "You never let people tell you what to do. Remember that time they were going to widen Blackberry Lane and everyone was going to lose five feet from their yards, so you led a big protest and they stopped? Do that here."

"I'm afraid I was a lot younger and had a lot more energy back then, Margaret." Gran leaned her head against the back of the couch and closed her eyes. "And I don't think I can bear to hear about one more thing I'm not allowed to do."

"But maybe if you talked to him . . ."

"Please. Don't hound me."

Margaret sat back, hurt. She wasn't *hounding*

Gran, she was trying to rev her up. Trying to make Gran stand up for herself, the way she always told Margaret *she* should. But there Gran was, leaning back in that exhausted way with her eyes closed as if she didn't have the energy to do *anything* anymore.

Tears of frustration prickled behind Margaret's eyes.

"I hate Mr. Whiting," said Roy.

"Me, too," said Margaret.

"Me, three," said Gran. Then her eyes shot open and she actually laughed. "Listen to me," she said, sitting up straight. "I sound like a child."

She was all energy again, filled with love and concern as she patted the couch on either side of her. "Come here, both of you," she said. "I'm sorry I've upset you." She put an arm around each of them as they settled down next to her. Roy immediately slumped against her, but Margaret held herself stiff. "You mustn't worry about me. I'm fine, really. I don't know what gets into me. I go along perfectly happy for days at a time, and then something happens to set me off. Seeing your shining faces makes me think of how much Tad would love to be here, enjoying you the way I am."

"Are you going to die of a broken heart?" said Roy in a small voice.

"No, Roy, I'm not." Gran's voice was firm. "I

may have to live with one for a while, but I'm definitely not going to die of one. I was married to your grandfather for a long time, so of course I'm sad. But I think that if I missed him one iota less than I do, that would be more sad, don't you?"

She looked at Margaret's glum face, and then at Roy's, and laughed. "Look at you both!" she said. "You're two of the gloomiest cheerer-uppers I've ever seen. Come on, what would you like to do this afternoon?"

Roy was caught up in her new mood immediately. "Can we go to the zoo?" he said. "The one you took me to when I was little?"

"What, you're not little anymore?" Gran laughed. "I don't see why not. How about you, Margaret?"

Margaret hesitated. It was scary, the way Gran kept changing. One minute she was sad, the next minute she was happy. Margaret wasn't sure she could trust this new mood, but there *was* something she wanted to do, more than anything. "Could we maybe drive by Blackberry Lane?" she said tentatively. "Maybe the new people will let Roy and me climb the tree fort."

The minute she said it, she knew it was a mistake, because Gran's face fell again. Oh, she *wished* Gran would try it, just *try* it. It would do her good. Gran missed the old house, too, Margaret could tell. It would be so wonderful to drive by. Margaret had spent so much time there, it was as familiar to her as her own house. She loved the slanting floors upstairs, and the wide screen porch that wrapped around two sides of the house. She loved the round window at the bottom of the stairs that the sun shone through as dependably as a clock. Tad said the stairs could tell time. "Yep, it's one o'clock," he would say in the summer when the sun hit the second step from the bottom. And "Uh-oh, almost lunchtime," when it shone on the fourth step in the winter.

If Gran drove past the house, it would make her feel better—Margaret knew it would. But she wasn't going to. Margaret's shoulders sagged as Gran turned to stare blankly out the window.

"Oh, I don't know. . . ." Her voice trailed off. "To tell you the truth, I'm a bit afraid of seeing Blackberry Lane again."

It was too hard, Margaret thought. It was just too hard. Gran was like the sun on a windy day— shining bright one minute, hidden behind a cloud the next.

She looked down at her watch now and jumped to her feet, as if surprised. "My goodness, I didn't realize how late it was. You children must be starving." She left the room quickly. She's running away, Margaret thought, watching her. Running away from me. "I'll go wash my hands,"she said over her shoulder, "then we'll have lunch."

Roy and Margaret looked at each other without speaking as they listened to Gran's footsteps in the hallway and then her bedroom door closing.

"It wasn't me this time," Roy said quickly.

"It wasn't anyone," said Margaret bitterly. "It was Gran."

"Do you think she's crying again?" he said.

"You heard her. She's fine." Margaret got up and started to move restlessly around the room, picking up a magazine, then throwing it down. Taking one of Gran's glass animals off the shelf, then putting it back. She stopped by Gran's desk and stared down at her gloves.

"She's fine," she said again.

Roy watched her for a minute, then pulled his notebook out of his pocket and rested it on his knees. "How do you think you spell that?" he said.

"Spell what?" Margaret picked up one of Gran's gloves and frowned.

"Iota. Do you think it's spelled the way it sounds?"

"How should I know? I don't even know what it means," she said impatiently. She shoved her hand into Gran's glove and then stared at it, amazed. How could Gran's glove fit her hand? Shouldn't it be much too big? Was Gran shrinking? Disappearing, right in front of Margaret's eyes?

"I don't know what it means, either," said Roy. "That's why I want to look it up." He looked at Margaret expectantly, waiting for an answer. But it never came. When she finally looked up, he was gone.

Chapter 4.

The sun shining in her eyes woke Margaret up the next morning. She jumped out of bed and pulled on some shorts and a T-shirt, then slipped her feet into her sandals and ran a comb through her hair. *She* knew how to get this day off to a good start. She knew exactly how.

She ran down the hall and was about to head into the kitchen but then stopped. "Gran?" Margaret walked slowly into the living room. "Are you okay?"

Gran turned away from the picture window and smiled. "Good morning, Margaret. Come sit down." She patted the couch next to her. "I'm watching the birds on the feeder. We seem to have a family of cardinals."

"You're still in your pajamas," Margaret said. "You never come to breakfast in your pajamas."

"I do now, actually, from time to time," said Gran. She smiled vaguely. "Without Tad to cook breakfast for, or the garden to look after, there's really no reason to get dressed as early as I used to, is there?"

"But what about our walk?" It was silly, Margaret knew it was silly. But her eyes were suddenly stinging like mad. "We always took a walk first thing in the morning, remember? I thought maybe we could today."

"Oh, but we can't walk around here," said Gran.

"Why not?"

"Look at it, for Heaven's sake!" Gran swept her arm across the window, as if to draw Margaret's attention to the horrible scene outside. But all Margaret saw were people. There were three women in bright jackets and sweatpants walking quickly down the middle of the street, carrying small weights in their hands. Their arms were pumping briskly at their sides. Four men jogging toward them from the opposite direction parted and ran around them on either side like a stream around a rock. The women laughed, and raised their weights in greeting.

"What's wrong with it?" said Margaret, bewildered. "Those people are walking."

"That's not walking," said Gran. "Walking is being out in the country, surrounded by the fields and the sky, with nothing more than the scent of honeysuckle for company, and the lowing of cows in the distance. . . ." Her voice trailed off, and the way she looked, sitting there on the couch by herself, so small and alone inside her fluffy bathrobe, Margaret knew, she absolutely *knew*, that Gran was having the balloon feeling. She was floating higher and higher into the sky away from them, with nothing to tie her down. She didn't have the twins to push a book into her lap and demand that she read it to them, or Claire with her doelike eyes, asking if she'd play house . . . no one to stop her from disappearing forever.

She needed a friend. And Margaret was going to find her one.

Without another word, she turned on her heel and marched into the kitchen. Roy was at the table, reading.

"Come on," she said, slapping his book closed as she passed. "We've got work to do."

"What kind of work?" said Roy. He jumped up and followed her out onto the stoop. By the time he caught up with her, she was looking up and down the street with her hands on her hips and a frown on her face.

"We've got to make some friends," she said.

"What do we need friends for? We're only going to be here until Saturday."

"Not for us—for Gran." She pointed to the

house across the street. "Who lives in two-ten?"

"I don't know, but it's probably a lady. Gran said there were about fifty ladies for every man here, remember?"

"That's because women live longer than men. Come on." Margaret jumped down off the stoop and headed for the gate.

"What are you going to do?" asked Roy, running after her.

"I'm going to go over there and knock on the door."

He stopped, and his mouth fell open. "You can't *do* that," he called after her.

"I have to."

"But you don't even know them." He hesitated, then ran to catch up to her again. "What are you going to say?"

"I'll say we want to introduce ourselves. I'll bring her something." Margaret didn't look at him. "I don't know."

"Bring her what?" insisted Roy. He was leaping around in front of her like a sheepdog trying vainly to stop the flock from plunging off the edge of a cliff. "How can we know what she likes if we don't even know her?"

"I don't know, something like . . ." They stopped in front of the picket fence in front of number 210.

Margaret looked around the small yard in front of them. "Like these." She bent down and grabbed a fistful of yellow flowers from the bed inside the fence. "These are perfect."

"Those are hers!" shrieked Roy. He looked around frantically over his shoulder as if to see from which direction the police would arrive. "The lady in number two-ten!"

"So? If she planted them, she must like them, right?" Margaret held the healthy clump up and made a few adjustments. "They're perfect," she announced, and opened the gate.

"Margaret!"

She didn't turn around.

She didn't know what she was going to say, she realized as she headed up the walk. But she had to say *something*, didn't she? If Gran didn't make some friends soon, she was going to end up sitting inside the house all day in her pajamas, looking at the birds, for Heaven's sake. Gran, who used to say, "If God had meant for us to stay inside, he wouldn't have made the sky."

"Wait for me!" Margaret heard Roy's frantic whisper behind her as she put her finger on the doorbell. She put her ear against the door.

"Hurry up!" she said, flapping her hand. "Someone's coming!"

Roy barely had time to reach her side before the door was opened by a frail white-haired woman leaning on a cane.

"Hello!" Margaret said in a loud voice. She thrust the bouquet out in front of her so quickly that it almost hit the woman on the nose. "These are for you."

"Why, thank you," the woman said. If she was surprised, she didn't show it, but reached out to take the flowers, as commanded. Her wispy white hair was standing out around her head like dandelion fluff, and her bright brown eyes were half-closed, she was smiling so hard. "I love yellow flowers," she said in a pleased voice.

"I thought you might." Margaret shot Roy a triumphant look before turning back to the lady and sticking out her hand. "I'm Margaret Mack, and this is my cousin Roy Parker. My father and his mother are brother and sister."

Having done with her half of the introduction, she jabbed Roy in the side to speak.

"Hello," he said cautiously.

"We're visiting our grandmother, Elizabeth Mack," said Margaret. She got a firm grip on Roy's arm. He was ready to bolt at a moment's notice, she could tell. "She sent us to invite you to a tea party. She really wants to meet you."

"She does?" said Roy.

"Well, isn't this nice. . . ." The woman was beaming at them now, her head wobbling gently like a doll on the dashboard of a car. It looked as if they might stand there for quite some time.

"What's *your* name?" Margaret prodded helpfully.

"Of course, how silly of me." She held out a tiny hand. She had gnarled fingers and huge knuckles, but her grip was surprisingly strong. "I'm Nelly Tudley and I'm very pleased to meet you."

They shook hands all around very politely. Then Mrs. Tudley said, "Won't you come in?"

"We'd love to," said Margaret, ignoring the alarmed look on Roy's face as she pulled him firmly into Mrs. Tudley's front hall. She could feel him glaring at her as they followed along behind Mrs. Tudley, who was making her way slowly into the living room, talking.

"We don't get to see many young people around here," she said cheerfully. "I wish my grandchildren could visit more often, but they live way over on the other side of the country. In California."

"That's too bad," said Margaret. She stopped and looked around. "Your living room's exactly like Gran's, except she has her couch over there"—she waved her hand toward the fireplace—"and book shelves over there, where you have the piano. And her walls are yellow."

"It's funny, isn't it, living in a house that's exactly like everyone else's," said Mrs. Tudley. "I never quite get used to it. I'm sure your grandmother feels the same way. Please, sit down."

Margaret plopped down and settled herself comfortably into the cushions. Roy perched on the edge of the couch next to her, and keeping his back very straight and his eyes fixed on Mrs. Tudley, started to pinch Margaret's thigh with small, painful pinches.

"So!" said Margaret. She jumped sideways to the other end of the couch and pulled a cushion down between them. She knew he was trying to get her attention, but she wasn't going to look at him because she knew he'd only start making faces about leaving. And they had work to do. "How are you, Mrs. Tudley?"

"This is such a lovely surprise," Mrs. Tudley said again. She was nodding and beaming at them as if there was nothing out of the ordinary about two children she'd never seen before, scrambling around on her couch, attacking each other. She bent over a vase on the coffee table that was filled with the same kind of yellow flowers she was holding, and began fitting the new ones into it while she talked. "It's so kind of your grandmother to invite me. We've never met, but I heard that she lost her husband shortly after they moved in. I knocked on her door several times to extend my condolences, but she wasn't home."

"She was probably hiding," said Margaret.

"Yes, she's very shy," said Roy.

"No, she's not, Roy."

"Margaret . . ."

"Oh, there's no need to be embarrassed." Mrs. Tudley gave a tinkly laugh. "I hid, too, after my husband died. There's no telling what a person will do when they lose a spouse after many years. I'll never forget my sister-in-law when *her* husband died. She was in total control until we got to the cemetery. Then she threw herself across Arnold's coffin and started yelling, 'Take me! Please, God, take me!'"

She stuck the last flower in the vase and gave the crowded arrangement a pleased pat. "It was dreadful."

"Did he?" said Roy.

"Oh, no. She's quite happily remarried." Mrs. Tudley sat down and rested her cane against the arm of her chair. "They just got back from a cruise to Alaska."

"That would have been amazing." Roy sounded disappointed, as if he would have been interested in seeing the skies part and Arnold's widow snatched from the earth by a huge hand.

"Our grandfather's name was David," said Margaret, steering the conversation back on track. "But everyone called him Tad. He was the youngest of five boys." She paused. "Get it? Tadpole?"

"I knew a butcher once named David," said Mrs. Tudley. "He had the most beautiful hands. My husband's name was Livingston. Livingston Dudley Tudley."

"Livingston Dudley Tudley?" said Margaret.

"That's nice," said Roy. "It rhymes."

"Oh, but it wasn't nice at all," said Mrs. Tudley. "He hated it. We all called him Tubby."

"Tubby Tudley?" said Margaret. She could hear herself repeating everything Mrs. Tudley said, but she couldn't help it. Tubby Tudley sounded like a bathtub toy.

"Why, was he fat?" said Roy.

"Roy!"

"That's all right, dear, I don't mind." Mrs. Tudley beamed at Roy encouragingly. "Yes, Roy, Tubby was very tubby."

"That's too bad," Roy said. "He could die of a heart attack."

"He's already dead," Margaret muttered out of the corner of her mouth. She wished she hadn't pulled the cushion down. She would have loved to get a hold of *his* thigh.

"Oh, Tubby didn't mind," said Mrs. Tudley. "Being fat wasn't nearly as bad a thing in those days as it is today, you know. Tubby was a happy, portly little man."

She leaned toward them suddenly. "Have you ever seen those wooden dolls that are cut through the middle and have a smaller doll inside, and then a smaller doll inside that, and so on?"

"I have one of those," said Margaret. "It's Chinese."

"Well, that's what Tubby looked like, except he was English." Mrs. Tudley leaned back in her chair with a satisfied expression on her face. "Everyone was amazed at what a wonderful dancer he was. Fat people often are, you know. They're very light on their feet."

"That sounds impossible," said Margaret. She pictured a little fat man suspended from the ceiling in a bouncing baby swing, doing a graceful tap dance, and frowned.

"It does, indeed," said Mrs. Tudley. "But it's true."

"Did you know that more than half the people in the United States today are overweight?" Roy said.

"Are they?" Mrs. Tudley sounded suitably impressed. "That sounds like a rather alarming statistic, doesn't it?"

"That's why so many people are dying of heart attacks."

"Roy talks about health and infections a lot." Margaret shot him a daggerlike look. "That's interesting, what you said about dancing, Mrs. Tudley," she said firmly. "Gran and Tad loved to dance. They went dancing all the time."

"Oh, so did Tubby and I. We were quite the couple on the dance floor. Tubby loved to spin."

"Spin?"

"Oh, yes. Around . . . and around . . . and around." Mrs. Tudley stopped and leaned toward them again, speaking in a low voice as if worried that Tubby might overhear. "Actually, I was sick in the ladies' room more than once. But I never told Tubby. He was having such a lovely time, poor dear."

"Maybe you and Gran could go dancing together," said Roy.

"Girls don't dance with girls," said Margaret, thinking she never should have invited him along because he said such ridiculous things.

But Mrs. Tudley didn't seem to think it was ridiculous. All she did was laugh. "At our age, they do. They have to. There aren't enough men to go around. Maybe your grandmother would like to join our dance group at the Recreation Center. We learn a new dance every week. I believe next week is the tango."

"She'd like that," Margaret lied. "Maybe you could ask her."

"I like to dance," said Roy.

"We're not talking about you, Roy," Margaret said, giving him her most ferocious glare, the one that always made Claire clamp her mouth shut immediately in the most satisfying way. But it didn't work with Roy. He just kept on talking.

"I'm going to take dance lessons at Miss Porter's when I'm ten," he said. "The girls have to wear gloves and the boys have to wear a jacket and tie and everything."

Margaret put her head in her hands and slid down into the couch. Trying to keep this conversation on track was like steering a bumper car. Just when she had it on a straight course, Roy sent it careening off in another direction.

"Good for you," said Mrs. Tudley. "I think it's a very good idea for young people to take dancing lessons. Both of my children did. I was worried I might have to give it up after I broke my hip two years ago, but the doctor said it's actually the perfect therapy."

"If you'd like to talk about your aches and pains a bit, that's okay," said Margaret, looking up.

"Aches and pains? Oh, dear me, no." Mrs. Tudley gave a delighted laugh. "I have no complaints at all, other than a touch of osteoporosis, and that won't kill me."

"Is that why you have that big circle between your legs?" said Roy.

"Roy!"

But Mrs. Tudley laughed again. "It's all right, Margaret. Roy's right. I do have a circle between my legs. It's gotten so I'm beginning to feel like a cowboy."

She stuck her little bowed legs out in front of her for them to inspect.

"I can't believe you said that," Margaret said in a faint voice. But it was amazing. Roy was right. She could have pushed a basketball through the gap between Mrs. Tudley's legs.

"My legs are getting bowed, and I'm shrinking," Mrs. Tudley was saying. "I've lost four inches already."

She sounded pleased, as if shrinking was what she had in mind and she was proud of doing it so well.

"When you're as tall as me, maybe we could dance together," said Roy.

"Why, Roy . . ." Mrs. Tudley blinked and lowered her feet slowly to the floor. Her eyes were suspiciously bright. "That's the nicest thing anyone's said to me in years," she said.

The room was suddenly too hot and too close for Margaret. "It was nice meeting you, Mrs. Tudley," she said quickly. She stood up, stuffed the cushion back into the couch, then grabbed Roy's arm. "We have to be going now. We have a lot of other calls to make."

"So soon?" Mrs. Tudley's head started to shake more noticeably, as if buffeted by wind. "I was about to offer you something to eat."

"That would be nice," said Roy.

He would have sat down again, but Margaret kept a firm grip on him as she headed for the door. "No, thank you," she called. "We're not hungry. I'll let you know when the party is going to be."

"I'll look forward to it," called Mrs. Tudley.

"Goodbye!"

Margaret slammed the door before Mrs. Tudley could reply. Then she turned on Roy furiously. "I can't believe you. We go to meet someone to try to make a friend for Gran, and you end up making her cry!"

Roy held his hands up in front of him. "All I said was that I would dance with her."

"You can't say things like that to old people," said Margaret. "You can't say anything too nice or too sad. You can't talk about their husbands, or what they did in the past, or where they lived, or anything."

"What *can* you talk about?"

"*You* can't talk about anything!" shouted Margaret, stomping down the path. "You just listen. If I let you talk, you'll start asking questions and talking about fat people and heart attacks, and the next thing you know, they'll be crying."

"Mrs. Tudley didn't seem old," said Roy. "She was fun."

"Yearwise she's old, okay? Too old to want an eight-year-old for a friend." She pushed open the gate and started down the sidewalk.

"She liked me," said Roy stiffly. "I could tell."

"We don't *want* her to like you," said Margaret. "We want her to like *Gran.*"

There was a stubborn silence behind her as they headed for the next house. Then Roy said, "How can they like her if they don't even know her?"

Margaret stopped and turned around. "That's why I'm inviting them to a party," she said. She enunciated each word carefully so he would understand how dense he was being. "To meet her."

"I already know that," said Roy. "But what's Gran going to say when they show up?"

Looking at his calm face, she could feel all of her resolve oozing out of her. She never should have asked him to come with her. The way he was always examining things and asking questions only made her feel doubtful. And there wasn't time for her to feel doubtful. Before she left, she was going to make sure Gran's house was full of people, whether Gran liked it or not.

"Fine. I'll go by myself." She pushed open the gate to the next house and walked toward the front door.

Roy materialized at her side like a ghost. "You don't have a present this time."

"Too bad."

She hesitated at the bottom of the steps.

"We're going to have to give them food," said Roy. "Did you think about that?"

Margaret put her finger on the doorbell. "First things first," she said, and pushed.

Chapter 5.

"Maybe they're not home," said Roy hopefully. "Maybe we should come back tomorrow."

Margaret put her ear against the door. They were home, all right. She could hear a faint sound from somewhere inside. A television, maybe.

"There's someone in there," she said determinedly. "Come on." She jumped off the steps and bolted around the corner of the house.

"Hey! Wait for me!" Roy jumped blindly off the stoop after her. He limped noisily around the corner of the house, with blood beading up along a new scratch on his shin. Margaret turned to look at him from where she was peering through the glass door on the back terrace, and put a finger up to her lips.

"Shh," she said quietly. She pressed her face back against the glass.

"You can't do that," Roy said. He limped over to her. "You're being a peeping Tom. You could be arrested."

"You've got to see this!" Margaret whispered. "You won't believe it."

Roy inched up next to her and peered fearfully through the glass.

There was a woman inside. She was sitting on a stool in the middle of the room. Her feet were planted wide apart and her hands were resting on her knees. She had on bright green sneakers and a flowing purple dress. But they couldn't see what her face looked like, because she had a bucket over her head.

A gray plastic bucket. Muffled, droning sounds were coming from underneath it.

"What do you think she's doing?" whispered Roy.

"I don't know." Margaret's voice was hushed.

They watched in silence for a minute. Then Roy said, "Do you think she's stuck?"

"No."

More silence.

"Maybe she's bald, and she doesn't want anyone to know," he said.

Margaret dragged her eyes away to look at him. This was the weirdest thing she had ever seen.

"Maybe she's trying to kill herself," she said. She

paused dramatically. "By suffocation," she added, and was pleased to see Roy's eyes grow huge.

"Do you think she could?" he said.

"I don't know." They turned their faces back to the window again. "It doesn't look like there's very much air in there," said Margaret.

Suddenly, the woman coughed. The bucket wobbled around on her broad shoulders, and then stopped. She sat up straighter and moved her feet closer together. The droning noise started up again.

Margaret let out a puff of air that left a perfect circle on the glass. She didn't know whether she should run inside and pull the bucket off the woman's head—thereby saving her life—or simply run. It might be kind of interesting, saving a person's life.

But what if the woman *was* trying to suffocate, and her eyes were bulging out and her face was all blue and swollen? What if she had been in a terrible accident, and her face was so scarred that she wore the bucket so that no one would see? What if . . . ?

When the woman coughed again, Roy clutched her arm. This time, it was a whole string of coughs. When the bucket began to wobble again, the woman reached up with both hands to steady it. Except this time, she didn't just steady it, she lifted it clean off her head.

Roy let out an ear-piercing shriek.

The woman turned to them with an astonished face and caught them staring at her with their noses pressed up against her door. It was hard to tell who was more surprised.

The woman recovered first. She stood up and came toward them, a mountain on the move. Everything about her was big: her bright red hair piled up on her head like a whirl of whipped cream, her shelflike bosom, and her face. Her face was enormous. Her cheeks were as round as hamburger buns and her chins led down to her neck in steps. Her mouth—the biggest, widest mouth Margaret had ever seen—was open wide.

Margaret couldn't tell whether she was laughing or shouting until she opened the door and Margaret, who was still leaning against it, frozen, fell into her outstretched arms. When she had finally pushed herself up and away from the woman's massive arms to stand on her own two feet again, she glared at the woman's amused face indignantly. "It's not funny," she said. "You almost gave Roy a heart attack."

The woman made a string of loud barks that sounded like a seal. "I can't imagine what you children must be thinking. You should see your faces."

"We thought you were suffocating," said Roy.

"It *was* hot in there," she said. She fanned her

face with her hands, making the bracelets on her arms tinkle together like wind chimes. There were necklaces around her neck, too, and dangling earrings that matched her dress.

"Well, I'm glad you're still with us, Roy," she said cheerfully. "There's a perfectly reasonable explanation, I assure you. Come in, come in. Let me explain."

Margaret already *was* in, and Roy didn't look as if he was sure he wanted to be. But when the woman pulled him in gently and shut the door, he immediately tilted his head and started sniffing the air like a hound dog. "You smell good," he said approvingly.

"Bay rum. I've worn it for years."

"Bay rum's for men," said Margaret. "Tad wore it."

"Tad's our grandfather," said Roy.

"*Was* our grandfather," Margaret said. "He's dead. That's why we're here."

"Dead?" The woman slapped a hand to her chest dramatically. "You mean now? At your house?"

"No, no," said Margaret quickly. "He died almost a year ago."

"Oh, thank goodness." The woman set the wind chimes going again. "I thought you were having a medical emergency, looking for a nurse or someone, with your noses pressed against my door like that."

Margaret had the grace to blush.

"No need to be embarrassed." The woman was already heading back into the room. "Come and sit down. Roy what?"

"Roy Parker."

"And you?"

"I'm Margaret Mack. We're cousins."

"Nice to meet you, Roy and Margaret. I'm Agatha Nightingale." She sat down and waved a hand toward the couch. "Please. No standing on ceremony."

Whether it was because of her open, smiling face, or her familiar smell, it suddenly felt like they were old friends.

"If you don't need me to help resuscitate your grandfather," Mrs. Nightingale said when they were settled, "what *do* you need me for?"

"We came to invite you to a party at our grandmother's," Margaret said. "Mrs. David Mack. She lives across the street."

"Ah, yes, the renegade."

"She's very nice," said Roy defensively. Then he frowned. "What's a renegade?"

"Someone who goes against the grain," said Mrs. Nightingale. "And I'm sure she is. Nice, I mean. I admire her spirit. Sheets on the line, banana peels in the garden." She barked again. "You don't have to look so surprised. We all know everything about one another at Carol Woods. And I'd say being a renegade runs in your family, Roy. Most people around here use the front door to extend party invitations."

She could have been mad at them, but she wasn't. She thought it was funny. Margaret suddenly liked her very much.

"We rang," she said, "but no one answered."

"Ah, yes." Mrs. Nightingale bent down and picked up the bucket. "That's because I was under this."

Margaret had forgotten all about the bucket. Now she looked at it in wonder. "What were you doing under there?" she said.

It was Mrs. Nightingale's turn to look embarrassed. "You may find this hard to believe, but I was trying to learn how to sing."

"Under a bucket?" said Margaret and Roy in unison.

"I know, it sounds ridiculous." Mrs. Nightingale sighed. "But you're looking at a desperate woman. I've promised myself for a year now that I would sing at the Recreation Club's karaoke evening, and tomorrow night, I'm going to do it!" She pounded a fist into her palm.

"What's karaoke?" said Roy.

"It's where you get up on a stage, and they hand

you a microphone and put on some music, and you sing."

"How can a bucket teach you how to sing?" said Margaret.

"Several weeks ago I saw a picture in the newspaper of a singing class in Korea," said Mrs. Nightingale. "All of the students had buckets over their heads, and the caption said that by listening to the sound of their own voices, the students were learning how to sing. So I thought, Why not give it a try?"

"It kind of makes sense," Margaret said doubtfully.

Roy was eyeing the bucket as if it was an intriguing scientific experiment. "What's it like under there?" he said.

Mrs. Nightingale held it out to him. "Be my guest."

He took it very gingerly and lowered it over his head as solemnly as if he were an astronaut about to hurtle into outer space.

"What's it like?" said Margaret.

"You don't have to shout. I can hear you." There was a short silence. Margaret knew he was probably looking around, examining it. Finally, he said, "Actually, it's kind of interesting."

"Roy finds everything interesting," Margaret

said to Mrs. Nightingale, rolling her eyes. Then to Roy, "Sing something."

There was another pause, then Roy's muffled voice. "Ninety-nine bottles of beer on the wall, ninety-nine bottles of beer—"

"Oh, for Pete's sake. We'll be here all day," said Margaret. She snatched the bucket off Roy's head and lowered it over her own. It smelled of plastic and bay rum.

"Testing one, two, three. Testing . . ."

It was amazing. It actually worked. There was nowhere else for her voice to go but back into her own ears.

She lifted the bucket off and handed it to Mrs. Nightingale. "It just might work," she said.

"It hasn't so far," said Mrs. Nightingale. "And I'm running out of time."

"I bet you can sing," said Roy encouragingly. "Everyone can sing."

"Not me. I'm tone-deaf. Completely, utterly tone-deaf."

"How about 'Happy Birthday'?" he insisted. "I bet you can sing that."

Mrs. Nightingale didn't bother to argue. She simply opened her mouth and sang.

It was incredible. The words were the ones for "Happy Birthday," but the tune didn't sound anything like it. It didn't sound like any tune Margaret had ever heard before. She could feel her face puckering up the way it did when she sucked on a lemon. It was a good thing Mrs. Nightingale was tone-deaf, or she would have been pretty miserable under the bucket.

Margaret looked at Roy. He had his hands over his ears and his shoulders hunched, as if someone was about to hit him. They sat there frozen like twin gargoyles until Mrs. Nightingale sang the last, horrible note. Then Roy took his hands away from his ears.

"That wasn't so bad," he said kindly.

"Yes, it was," said Margaret. "It was terrible."

"When I was a girl, every time I opened up my mouth to sing, my brother yelled, 'I'm telling!'" said Mrs. Nightingale.

"That was mean," said Roy.

"Yeah, but you can't really blame him," said Margaret.

"It's not easy, having a voice like mine and a name like Nightingale, let me tell you." With her bright red lips and shiny red cheeks, she looked like a clown who can change from funny to sad in an instant. She was sad now. "All my life, all I've ever wanted was to sing on a stage in front of an audience, and hear them applaud," she said wistfully.

I wouldn't count on the applauding part, Margaret was tempted to say. But she couldn't. Not with the way Mrs. Nightingale looked.

"You could sing to Roy and me," she said instead. "We wouldn't mind, would we, Roy?"

"Not that much."

"You're both very sweet." Their sympathy seemed to cheer her up, because she was suddenly her smiling, jovial self again. "Thank you, but no. It's karaoke or nothing."

"Maybe they can turn up the music really loud, to drown you out," said Roy.

"And we can come and clap, so people'll think you sound good," said Margaret. "We'll ask Mrs. Tudley, too. And Gran. We'll all clap."

"Then no one will be able to hear you," finished Roy. "It'll be great."

Mrs. Nightingale threw her head back and laughed so hard, everything on her jiggled. "I don't know whether to be insulted or encouraged," she said at last. "But I'll do it."

"Yippee!" shouted Roy, jumping to his feet.

"Oh, I'm so excited," said Margaret. It felt so good to try to cheer somebody up and actually have it work for a change that she jumped up, too, and was hugging Mrs. Nightingale around the neck before she remembered they were strangers. She drew back, embarrassed.

But Mrs. Nightingale had already turned to Roy.

"Come on, one from you, too, Roy." She enveloped him in an enthusiastic embrace, from which he emerged red-faced but pleased.

"There can be no formalities among the three of us if you're going to help launch me on my new career," said Mrs. Nightingale. "Now, you two had better run along. I have lots of work to do, and not much time."

"Gran can have her party after the karaoke," said Margaret as Mrs. Nightingale opened the door. "It'll be perfect."

"I don't know whether you'll all be consoling me or congratulating me, but it will be nice to have the company," called Mrs. Nightingale from her front stoop.

Roy was about to lead the way through the gate when Margaret stopped. She couldn't leave without asking one more question. "Wait a minute," she said quickly. She turned and ran back to the bottom of the steps. "Mrs. Nightingale?" she said uncertainly.

"Yes, Margaret?"

Margaret took a deep breath. "When your brother was mean to you, did it make you hate him for the rest of your life?" she said in a rush.

"Ronald? Why, I adore him. He's one of my best friends. Why do you ask?"

"I don't know."

Mrs. Nightingale's face creased in an understanding smile. "I wouldn't worry if I were you," she said kindly. "Siblings are resilient creatures. If you've done something you're sorry for, I'm sure you'll make it up to them. You're a nice girl, Margaret, I can tell. "

Margaret felt as if a huge weight had been lifted off her shoulders. She was suddenly as light as air. "Thanks," she said. She smiled radiantly and ran back to join Roy out on the street.

"Tell your grandmother I'm looking forward to meeting her," Mrs. Nightingale called as they crossed the street.

"We will!" chorused Margaret and Roy.

"It certainly was a serendipitous event, meeting you two!"

"Same here," yelled Margaret. "See you tomorrow!"

"Ser-en-di-pi-tous," said Roy. He pulled out his notebook and slowed down so he could write. "That will be my longest word ever."

"It means lucky," said Margaret.

"How do you know?"

"I just do. Go ahead"—she executed a perfect cartwheel, then kept on walking—"look it up."

It did mean lucky, she thought happily. She could

feel it in her bones. Mrs. Nightingale was lucky to have met them, and they were lucky to have met Mrs. Nightingale.

She could hardly wait to introduce her to Gran.

Chapter 6.

"... and her husband's name was really Livingston Dudley Tudley ..."

"But they called him Tubby because he was fat."

"But he didn't mind," said Margaret, "because being fat wasn't so bad back then."

"Being overweight is never a good idea," Roy said.

"And Mrs. Nightingale was singing with a bucket over her head, because she's tone-deaf," said Margaret.

"You can imagine how hard it is on her with a name like Nightingale," said Roy.

They were standing side by side in front of Gran, soldiers reporting on a successful mission. She had been looking from one eager face to the other like a spectator at a tennis match. Now she put down the pen she'd been using to address an envelope, and smiled. "It sounds as if you two have had a very busy morning."

"They're really great, Gran," Margaret said. "You'll like them."

"Mrs. Tudley loves to dance," said Roy. "We told her you might want to go to her dance class at the Recreation Center."

Margaret pinched him, but it was too late. Two bright red spots appeared on Gran's cheeks. Her mouth flattened into a disapproving line.

"You're good to think of me, Roy," she said stiffly, "but I'm not so old yet that I view dancing with a bunch of old women in a cafeteria as something to look forward to."

Roy looked hurt.

The smile fell from Margaret's face. "That's not very nice, Gran," she said. "You don't even know Mrs. Tudley and Mrs. Nightingale."

"Yeah, and when Mrs. Tudley came over to say she was sorry about Tad, you hid," said Roy. "And she's shrinking."

"Don't you think you should at least give them a chance?" said Margaret. "Meet them a few times, and see if you like them?"

"I don't know. . . ." Gran picked up the envelope and looked at it thoughtfully in silence for a minute.

"I've been sitting here for a while, composing a letter to Mr. Whiting. If Tad were here, we'd have a good laugh over all these silly rules. But by myself . . . ?" She looked at Margaret with a stony face. "I'm afraid I don't have the energy for any of it right now, Margaret. I don't even feel like walking this to the mailbox, if it comes to that.

"Since you have so much energy, Roy, why don't *you* take it?" she said suddenly, holding out the envelope to him. "You might even want to take it directly to Mr. Whiting. Maybe he's another resident of Carol Woods I should get to know."

"Me?" Roy said. He took a step back. He was afraid to take the letter, Margaret realized, and hurt by the sarcastic tone in Gran's voice. "Why me?" he said helplessly.

For Margaret, it was the final straw. Here they were, trying their best to cheer Gran up and make her happy, and Mrs. Nightingale and Mrs. Tudley, full of sympathy and understanding for a person they didn't even know, and here was Gran, being mean and sarcastic about them all. Worst of all, she was deliberately being horrible to Roy, her own grandson, who was gentle and kind and never said a mean word to anyone.

Margaret snatched the envelope out of Gran's hand. She knew she was being rude, but she didn't care.

"I'll take it to him," she said abruptly, turning on her heel. "Come on, Roy."

He waited until they were outside to speak.

"Why can't we just put it in the mailbox?" he said, scurrying after her. "Why do we have to take it all the way to him? Mr. Whiting hates Gran. What if he yells at us?"

"So? Haven't you ever heard anyone yell before?" Margaret pushed the gate open with such energy, it flew back and hit Roy in the stomach.

"Hey! What are you mad at *me* for?" he said.

"She's brooding," said Margaret. She was stomping her feet so hard that little pieces of gravel were shooting out to either side like sparks. "She's sitting around like a chicken all day long, brooding."

"Are you sure?"

"You saw her!" said Margaret. "Everyone's trying as hard as they can, and all she does is act tired, and look out the window, and say 'I don't know' all the time. She's being mean about people she doesn't even know, and she's being mean to us. Her own grandchildren."

"No, I mean the chicken part," said Roy. "I mean, I think chickens are hens, but I don't think they brood. I think hens brood, but—"

"For heaven's sake, Roy! *Who cares?*" Margaret shouted. She halted and whirled around to face him so fast that he almost ran right into her. "I'm talking about Gran's attitude. There are lots of things to do around here, if she'd give them a chance. And the people are nice. No one's talking about their aches and pains like she said. They're all doing things. Everyone except Gran."

"I feel sorry for her," said Roy.

"Feeling sorry isn't doing her any good," said Margaret. "It's only making her feel more sorry for herself."

"Maybe she's scared."

"Of what?"

"I don't know. Maybe she's afraid she's next."

"Next for what?"

"Next to die."

"What?" The word was so unexpected, Margaret shook her head slightly, as if she wasn't sure she had heard him correctly. "What are you talking about? Gran's not dying."

"She might feel like she is," he said. "Tad died, didn't he? They were almost the same age. Maybe Gran thinks she's next."

"But Gran's in perfect health."

"Tad was, too, until he got sick."

Margaret couldn't think of a thing to say. Roy kind of had a point. Maybe Gran was afraid. Margaret was afraid sometimes, too. But she couldn't go around being afraid for the rest of her life, could she? That would be horrible.

Gran couldn't either.

"I don't care." She started to walk again. "She's got to try harder."

Roy walked along beside her. "When are we going to tell her she's having them over for a party?" he said.

"I don't know. Maybe we won't even have the stupid party." She stopped in front of the last house on the block and looked from the letter in her hand to the front door. "One-sixty. This is it."

"Let's slip it under the door and run," said Roy.

"Why should we run? We haven't done anything."

"We're related to Gran, that's why."

"Mr. Whiting doesn't know that," said Margaret. "We'll tell him a grouchy old lady we never saw before made us deliver it."

"And then we'll run?"

But they didn't have time to do anything. Before they even got to the door, it was flung open wide and a shrill voice shouted, "Get lost!"

Chapter 7.

"Now, now, Rolly, mind your manners." Mr. Whiting reached up and smoothed the feathers of the large gray bird on his shoulder. "That's no way to greet our visitors."

He wasn't at all what Margaret had expected. He was wearing a pale gray cardigan, a bow tie, and slippers. His thin white hair was slicked back from his face, and his curly eyebrows stuck out over his gentle eyes like wings. This was the mean, horrible Mr. Whiting?

"We're not visiting," she said. She held out Gran's letter. "We came to bring you this."

"Is that a parrot?" said Roy. He looked as if he had dropped any idea of fleeing, and was gazing up at Mr. Whiting's bird admiringly. "I've always wanted a parrot."

"Rolly is a cockatiel," said Mr. Whiting. He held Gran's letter in the air and squinted. "How nice. A letter from Mrs. Mack. At long last."

"How do you know who it's from?" said Margaret.

"I have to confess, I saw you coming," he said. He held up the binoculars that were hanging around his neck on a cord.

Margaret's eyes widened in shock. "You were spying on us!" she said indignantly.

"Actually, I was watching a flock of warblers," said Mr. Whiting. "But I did catch you in my sight, yes."

"Spying's sneaky," she said.

"In this case, it was strictly by accident, I assure you. I didn't mean to be sneaky. Just as I'm sure you didn't mean to litter when you threw your half-eaten Popsicle over your shoulder onto my lawn."

When Margaret's face fell, Mr. Whiting laughed gleefully. His laugh was almost as shocking as his spying. Mr. Whiting wasn't mean, he was sweet.

"Your sister's very fierce, isn't she?" he said to Roy.

"He's not my brother, he's my cousin," said Margaret. "And you're being mean to our grandmother."

"Mean to your grandmother?" said Mr. Whiting. "Why, we haven't even met. I knocked on her door two or three times, but she wasn't in, and she never attends our monthly Steering Committee meetings. How on earth have I been mean to her?"

"You sent her mean letters about your dumb old rules."

"But my dear young lady," he said. "Those were *form* letters. We send them to all the new residents when they seem to be doing something in violation of our rules. Surely, your grandmother doesn't think they're *my* rules.

"Tell them, Rolly," he said, turning to the bird and scratching its chest with his finger. "Tell them what a nice man I am."

"Come in! Come in!" Rolly shrieked. He stretched up to his full length and ruffled his feathers, as if preparing for liftoff.

"Does he bite?" said Roy.

"Absolutely not," said Mr. Whiting. "And neither do I. Rolly's right—come in. We need to clear this thing up."

"No, thank you," said Margaret. "We have to go."

"Nonsense. Roy wants to see my goldfish pond and my Siamese fighting fish." He looked at Roy and winked. "Don't you, Roy?"

"Oh, yes, please," said Roy. He slipped eagerly into Mr. Whiting's hall before Margaret could stop him. "Siamese fighting fish are beautiful."

"*Roy,*" she said meaningfully, but it was no use. He was already trotting down the hall behind Mr. Whiting like an obedient puppy. Margaret could hear his high voice asking questions as they disappeared.

By the time she caught up with them, they were in a sunny, humid room filled with plants. There was a wicker birdcage in one corner, and a tall perch next to a raised pond in the middle of the room. The pond had a fountain at one end, and lily pads. Roy was leaning on the edge, peering eagerly into its depths.

"Look at that one—it's huge," he said, pointing. "And that one." He looked at Mr. Whiting. "Is the Siamese fighting fish in there, too?"

"Just a moment." Mr. Whiting bent down so that his shoulder was on a level with the perch and said, "Rolly?"

Rolly gave another shocking squawk, stepped nimbly onto the perch, and immediately started preening his feathers with his beak.

"Ethel is over here," said Mr. Whiting. From the edge of the pond he picked up a small bowl that had an iridescent blue fish floating inside. The fish had a huge, feathery tail like a fan, and fins that extended from one side of the bowl to the other.

"Is that where it lives?" said Margaret. "That bowl is much too small."

"Ethel is a 'she,' not an 'it,'" said Mr. Whiting.

"There's no room for her to swim," said Margaret stubbornly. "What does she do all day?"

"I don't know," said Mr. Whiting. He looked thoughtful. "What does any fish do all day, except dart around?"

"Ethel couldn't dart if she wanted to," said Margaret. "That looks like a horrible life."

"She's perfectly happy, I assure you," said Mr. Whiting, but he peered into the bowl with anxious eyes. "You are happy in there, aren't you, Ethel? That's my girl."

It was funny to see a grown man talking to a fish in a voice like the one people use to talk to babies. In spite of herself, Margaret smiled.

"They come in other colors, don't they?" said Roy. "I saw one once that was red and green."

"Each one is different," said Mr. Whiting. He put the bowl back down on the edge of the pond. "Wait just a moment. I want to show you something."

Roy turned to Margaret with a shining face when he left. "Isn't she beautiful?"

"How could you?" she said.

"What did I do?"

"We weren't even going to come in here, remember?" She turned her hot gaze to Ethel. "Look at her. How would you like to live like that?"

"But I think Mr. Whiting's right, Margaret," said Roy. "I've seen lots of Siamese fighting fish in pet stores. They're always in small bowls like that."

Margaret grabbed his arm. "When he comes back, we're leaving, do you hear me?"

"Bossy lady! Bossy lady! *Awwwwwwk!*" Rolly flapped his wings furiously and lifted awkwardly off his perch. Margaret and Roy jumped back as he hurtled through the air and landed on the edge of Ethel's bowl, tipping it over. Ethel shot out onto the edge of the pond and Rolly flew back up onto his perch, then sat there calmly craning his neck around to fuss with the feathers on his back as if nothing had happened.

Margaret and Roy were left with their mouths hanging open and water all over their feet, watching Ethel plastered to the edge of the pond, trying to breathe. The only part of her that was moving was her mouth.

It was opening and closing, opening and closing.

"She's going to die like that," Roy said frantically. "What should we do?"

"Get her back into the water, quick," said Margaret. She darted a look over her shoulder. "Hurry! He's coming."

"You do it. I'm afraid."

Margaret bent down. With both hands cradled together, she flipped Ethel's body up off its deathbed into the life-preserving waters below. There was a furious roiling commotion as twenty massive goldfish raced to eat at the same time.

When Mr. Whiting came back into the room waving a book in the air, she and Roy were staring at the calm, empty surface of the pond.

"If you like Ethel, my boy," he called, "wait until you see this!"

Roy took one look at the empty fishbowl lying on its side, then at Mr. Whiting coming toward them, and burst into tears.

Chapter 8.

"What's this?" said Mr. Whiting, stopping short. He looked from Roy, in tears, to the guilty expression on Margaret's face, to the bowl on the floor, and finally at Rolly. "Rolly," he said in a stern voice, "look what you've done. You've upset our poor guests, just when we were starting to get along."

He pulled a snowy white handkerchief out of his pocket and handed it to Roy. "Please don't be upset, or you'll make me feel even worse."

Margaret was still getting over the shock of Ethel. Now she looked at Mr. Whiting. "How did you know it was Rolly?" she said.

"I'm sorry to say that it's happened before," he said. His eyes under his bushy brows were so sad, she immediately felt sorry for him. "And it's all my fault. I should simply stop buying them, but I can't."

"What do you mean?" said Roy.

Mr. Whiting slowly picked up the bowl and put it back on the edge of the pond. He went and sat down on a chair, and patted the book in his lap. "Come take a look at this."

They stood on either side of him as he opened it. It was a photograph album. The page Mr. Whiting had opened to was covered with photographs of fish.

Siamese fighting fish. In bowls. Each one was slightly different from the one next to it. The following page was filled with fish, too. And the one after that. Margaret stared at them in amazement. There must have been twenty pictures of Siamese fighting fish, each in its tiny bowl, suspended forever, side by side.

And under every photograph, in faint, spidery letters, someone had written the same name. Ethel.

"I started it when she was so sick, you see," Mr. Whiting was saying. "She couldn't get out of bed, and she wanted something pretty to look at. One day when I was out buying her some flowers, I saw this one in a store window." He flipped back to the first page and pointed to the first picture. "Ethel number one. My wife was delighted. I put it on her bedside table, and she watched it all the time. After Ethel died, I just couldn't seem to stop buying them."

"Ethel the fish?" said Margaret.

"Ethel my wife."

"Oh." Margaret looked at him. "You named them all after your wife."

"You must think I'm a silly old man," he said. "You children are probably too young to understand what it's like to miss someone as much as I miss my wife."

Margaret thought about her dad. "A person doesn't have to be dead for you to miss them," she said.

"You're so right, Margaret." He looked at her approvingly and a glimmer of his good humor came back into his eyes. "I can see that you're as wise as you are strict."

"Gran misses Tad. She was used to being part of a couple, and I don't think she feels as if she fits in." She was surprised at how right the words felt. "That's why she hasn't come to any of your meetings."

"That's a pretty normal reaction," Mr. Whiting said sympathetically. "A lot of people in Carol Woods have recently lost someone, I'm afraid. That's why many of them live in a retirement community. But most of us adjust. Don't you worry, Margaret," he patted her hand. "I think your grandmother will recover. From what I've seen of all the rules she has broken, she's a feisty woman. When she feels better, I hope she joins the rest of us folks. We manage to have a pretty good time."

"Is Rolly short for Roland?" Roy piped in.

It was just like Roy to bring up a totally different subject, but this time Margaret was glad. Her eyes were suddenly stinging with tears.

"Yes, isn't that silly? It's a good thing my wife and I got along better than the fish and the bird, wouldn't you say?" When Mr. Whiting laughed, so did Roy and Margaret. "I'm a sentimental old fool, that's what I am. It's been two years now. I think maybe the time has come for me to stop sacrificing poor, defenseless fish, don't you?"

"Maybe you could get another kind of pet and name it Ethel," said Margaret. "Something Rolly can't kill."

"A cat, perhaps?" said Mr. Whiting.

"How about a ferret?" said Roy. "They're nice pets."

"Now, *there's* a picture for you." Mr. Whiting slapped his knee. "I'll have to show you a photograph of my wife sometime, Roy. She was a rather big woman. Boy, if she saw a skinny, wiggly thing like a ferret running around with her name, she'd have a good laugh."

He closed the book decisively. "No, the time has come. No more pets named Ethel. Now, can I offer you children a snack of some sort?"

"We'd better get home before Gran thinks you had us arrested," said Roy.

"It's that bad, is it?" said Mr. Whiting, opening his front door.

"Gran's a lot like Margaret," said Roy.

The expression on his face was so funny that Margaret had to laugh. Mr. Whiting laughed, too. "It's been kind of tough, being around the two of them, huh?" he said to Roy.

"You can say that again," said Roy glumly.

"I think maybe their barks are worse than their bites most of the time, don't you?" said Mr. Whiting.

"Yeah, but their barks can be pretty bad," said Roy. "Especially Margaret's."

"Roy," Margaret protested, but she didn't really mind. She was suddenly very happy. She had a bark, and she never even knew it. She growled at Roy all the way down the street.

• • •

"Are you going to tell Gran how nice he is?" said Roy, as they got near Gran's.

"Nope."

"Why not?"

"She won't believe me." Margaret turned into Gran's yard. "I'm going to let her find out for herself."

"How can she, if she keeps on hiding?"

"She can't hide at her own party."

"You *invited* him?"

"When you were in the bathroom."

"What did he say?"

"He said he looked forward to changing Gran's opinion of him."

"Oh, brother," said Roy.

"Am I really a lot like Gran?" she said, opening the front door.

Roy rolled his eyes and went in past her.

"How did it go?" Gran called. They found her in the kitchen, baking. The entire house smelled of gingerbread. "I was thinking of sending out the troops," she said. "You were gone for a long time."

"It didn't seem long," said Roy. He slid into a chair.

"It seemed short," said Margaret, sitting down across from him.

"He wasn't rude to you, was he?"

"Nope," said Roy.

"Not at all," said Margaret.

Gran looked from one to the other, suspicious. "Well, what was he like?" she said impatiently.

"You'll find out," said Margaret. "At your party."

"My party?" Gran said. "What party?"

Roy slid down in his chair until his eyes were level with the tabletop.

"The one you're having after we come back from karaoke at the Recreation Club tomorrow night,"

Margaret said. She was suddenly unafraid, and it felt great. "We're all going to listen to Mrs. Nightingale sing first."

"Tone-deaf Mrs. Nightingale," Gran said.

"Right."

Gran's eyes looked into hers. Neither of them said a word, they just stared. It was as if they were waging a silent battle. Finally, Gran said, "May I ask who's coming?"

Roy slid out of sight.

"Mrs. Tudley, Mrs. Nightingale, and Mr. Whiting," said Margaret. "And Roy and me, of course."

"Of course."

For a minute, there wasn't a sound in the room. And then Gran spoke in a light voice, and Margaret knew she had won.

"Then I guess we'd better talk about food."

Chapter 9.

In the end, it was Gran's idea to drive by Blackberry Lane. The minute Margaret woke up the next morning, she could feel that something had changed. The air was filled with a delicious smell. She sat bolt upright in her bed and sniffed. It was. It had to be.

"Gran!" she cried, bursting through the kitchen door. "Are you making blueberry pancakes from your secret recipe?"

Gran turned to smile at her from in front of the stove. "I thought that might rouse you," she said. "Blueberry pancakes with the last of the Blackberry Lane blueberries, and a sprinkle of cinnamon." They both laughed. "Set the table, would you, Margaret, and call Roy."

They had had a very festive breakfast, at the end of which Gran had made her amazing suggestion.

Now they were driving down the Post Road, halfway there.

"Look," said Margaret. "Motley's still has the bubble-gum machine in the window!"

"I saw him! I saw Mr. Motley!" Roy was bouncing up and down in the back seat. He craned his head around as Gran drove by. "I think he saw me!"

"We'll stop in there on our way back," said Gran. The fact that she didn't tell him to stop bouncing made Margaret realize how distracted Gran was. She was doing a bit of craning, herself. "I see Tabbot's finally got a new awning."

"Gino's Pizza . . . Lotsa Lace . . . The Little Book Worm . . ." Margaret reeled off the names as they went by. "Nothing's changed," she said happily.

"We haven't been gone *that* long," said Gran. "It's only been a year." But Margaret could tell she was excited, too. She was leaning forward with her hands clutching the steering wheel, peering through the windshield.

They turned right onto Lake Street and drove past Maple View Farms. Margaret was the first to spot the wall of lilacs that hemmed in the Whites' house, right before Gran and Tad's.

"We're here!" she said excitedly. She wished she could open the door and jump out. She wanted to run the rest of the way, up the driveway, across the front yard, over to Tad's Folly, and up the ladder, without stopping.

"Now, calm down, both of you," said Gran. Her cheeks were bright red. "I'm just going to drive by. If there's anyone in the yard, I might stop."

She turned slowly onto Blackberry Lane.

"You never saw the turret Tad made, did you, Roy?" said Margaret. "I bet they'll let us climb up there. You said they were nice people, right, Gran?" She gripped the back of the seat as they pulled up in front of the house. She barely felt Roy's fingers dig into her arm or Gran's car come to a sudden stop, she was so shocked.

There wasn't any tree fort. There wasn't even any tree. In its place was a two-story addition that jutted out into the front yard. It had huge windows and a balcony. The house wasn't white anymore, either. It was blue.

As they sat there staring, a young woman holding a baby on her hip came hurrying down the driveway toward them. "Mrs. Mack," she called, "what a pleasant surprise." She was smiling in at them through the open window. "It's so nice to see you. Mark and I were saying last night that we wanted to give you a call."

Gran's face when she turned to look at the young woman was so terrible, Margaret was afraid. She leaned forward and put her hand on Gran's shoulder.

"What have you done?" said Gran. Her voice was thin and high, as if it were pushing out through a small space from far away. "You've ruined it. You've absolutely ruined it."

"What do you mean?" The woman couldn't have looked more shocked if Gran had slapped her. She put her arm around her baby's back, as if to protect it. "Please. Let me explain—"

"We never would have sold it to you if we'd known you were going to destroy it. Never." Gran's voice was terrible to listen to. Margaret was trying to think of something she could say, some way to explain, so that the woman would stop looking as if she was going to cry, when Gran began to fumble blindly with the gear stick, darting frenzied looks into the rear-view mirror. Roy was frozen on the seat next to her.

Margaret met the woman's eyes in mute appeal.

"Mrs. Mack, wait." The woman put her hand on Gran's window. "You shouldn't drive when you're so upset."

But Gran didn't wait. She found reverse, and the car jerked backward and bumped against the curb on the opposite side of the road. Then she started forward, picking up speed as they pulled onto Lake Lane back toward the Post Road. Margaret turned around and saw the woman standing at the end of the driveway, staring after them.

"It's all right, it's all right," Gran kept saying. Whether she was talking to herself or them, Margaret couldn't tell. When they got to the Post Road, Gran brought the car to a full stop and rested her forehead on the steering wheel. Margaret and Roy sat silent, watching her.

"Gran?" Roy said hesitantly after a while. "Are you okay?"

"I'm fine." She looked up and blinked. "Don't worry. Everything's fine. I just need to get home."

She pulled out onto the Post Road in slow motion. They drove back past The Little Book Worm. Past Lotsa Lace, Gino's Pizza, and Mr. Motley's. All the places that had seemed so exciting only minutes before felt like nothing now. Margaret hardly looked at them. She was keeping her eyes fixed firmly on the road, willing the car to stay on the path—to get us home safely, please, and take good care of us even though you're a car and not a person, because Gran is upset.

And all the while, the thought was running through her mind that the apple tree being gone wasn't the most terrible thing. Or even Tad's Folly. No, the *most* terrible thing was how good the house had looked. It looked like it was happy. Like it was used to the people who lived there now, and didn't miss the ones who had lived there before.

If a house had feelings, Margaret realized, that was how the house on Blackberry Lane felt. And that was the most terrible thing of all.

• • •

"Where are you going?" said Roy.

"I'm going to see what Gran's doing." Margaret turned and looked back at him. The two of them had been sitting in the living room, playing a half-hearted game of cards, for more than an hour since they had got back. "We can't let her sit in there forever."

"What are you going to say?"

"I don't know."

Margaret walked down the hall and stopped in front of Gran's closed door. She took a deep breath, and knocked.

"Come in."

Gran turned to look at her from in front of her dressing table. She had brushed her hair and washed her face. She looked very calm.

In her mind, Margaret had been practicing what she would say, the magic words that would bring Gran back to them, the way she'd been at breakfast, before their terrible trip had driven her further away. But in the end, she could only say what was true.

"It looks great," said Margaret. She came into the

room and raised her voice. "That room they added to the house looks great."

Gran smiled with her mouth, but not her eyes. "It does, doesn't it? Tad always talked about adding on to the front of the house and putting in big windows. He said our windows didn't let in enough sun."

"Then he would like it, too." Margaret sat down on the edge of Gran's bed. They looked at each other in silence for a minute.

"Look at us," Gran said.

"Who? You and me?"

"You and me."

Gran got up, came over, and sat down next to Margaret. She took Margaret's hands in her own. "Holding on to a house that way. Why, it's only a house!" She shook her head slowly, as if she was just waking up and was amazed she hadn't seen it before. "It's as if we've been shipwrecked, Margaret, and here we are, clinging to the wreckage, crying. When all we have to do is stand up."

Gran stood up quickly and held her arms out to either side, to show how easy it was. "The water's only up to our knees." She sounded exhilarated, and Margaret could almost imagine for herself how it would feel to put your feet on firm sand when you thought you were drowning.

Gran sat down as suddenly as she had stood up.

"Oh, when I think of how I treated that young woman. The things I said. I must have been out of my mind. I have to write to her immediately and apologize. It must have upset her horribly."

"You told her they ruined it," Margaret said.

"I know I did. But it's theirs! It's not ours anymore, it's theirs. We have no right to expect it to stay the same." She was talking to Margaret and herself at the same time, chiding them both for having looked at it in any other way. "The time has come to let it go." She patted Margaret's leg. "It's understandable for me, I'm an old woman. But you're a child. You should be excited about change. That's what life is."

"It's not always so exciting," said Margaret. She was finally going to get to say what she had come here to talk about, and it came out in a torrent. "Sometimes it's terrible, Gran. Blackberry Lane's not the only thing that's changed. Everything has."

Gran sat very still and listened while Margaret told her about Wendy and Dad and the dominoes, and being mean to Claire, and Dad sending her to Gran's to get rid of her.

"But *you* weren't the one who was being a handful," said Gran. She held Margaret's face between her strong hands for a moment and looked into her eyes. "Roy heard it wrong, Margaret. Your father and I were talking about Claire."

"Claire?" said Margaret, dumbfounded.

"Yes. Your father said she'd been waking up every night, and whining to sleep in your room, and clinging to you horribly. I can see he was right. She's called here every day since you arrived, wanting to speak to you."

"Claire has?" Margaret had a sudden vision of Claire's huge, sad eyes. "Why didn't you tell me?"

"Your father and Wendy felt that you needed a break," said Gran. "And I agree."

"But Claire can't help it," Margaret said. She had a feeling close to panic, thinking about Claire alone at the other end of the phone. "She's only six."

"I know she is, and she's had a hard time, poor lamb. Imagine, Margaret, what it must be like to be three and have your father go off to work and not come home. He died of a heart attack in his office and she never saw him again."

Margaret could easily imagine it. What amazed her was that she'd never even tried before.

"As for your domino theory, that's very well put," Gran went on. "I can see it in my mind's eye. Your whole world fell about you, and I was too wrapped up in my own problems to help."

"You couldn't have done anything," Margaret said.

"We'll just have to take our dominoes and start over, won't we?" said Gran. "We even have some new ones to work with—Wendy and the girls, and one more Mack who may be coming into the world even as we speak. And who says we have to stick to family? What about Mrs. Nightingale and Mrs. Tudley?"

"*They're* going to be a part of it?"

"I don't see why not. You and Roy tell me they're wonderful. Speaking of wonderful, that reminds me." Gran stood up, full of her old vigor. "If we're entertaining tonight, we'd better get started on our wardrobe."

"What wardrobe?"

But Gran was already gone, moving briskly down the hall, humming. As she disappeared into a huge walk-in closet that smelled of cedar, she said to Margaret over her shoulder, "Call Roy."

Margaret ran to the end of the hall. "Roy!" she shouted at the top of her lungs, and ran back to Gran, who was thumbing rapidly through the hangers. There was an excited feeling in the air, as if they were on a shopping spree.

"If Mrs. Nightingale is the flamboyant woman you say she is," said Gran, "we'll have to do a little sprucing up for her performance. I know it's in here somewhere."

"What's wrong?" said Roy, running into the room.

Gran took a gray oval hat box that was tied up with a shiny black satin ribbon off a shelf and handed it to him. "You look through this. It's where I keep Tad's suspenders. Find a pair you like. They're probably too long, but I can always hitch them up. And here." As Roy dropped to his knees with the box in front of him, Gran dropped Tad's gray fedora on his head. "He would have liked you to have this."

He looked up at them and smiled. With his open face and lopsided smile, he reminded Margaret of someone. Then she knew who it was. "He looks like a miniature Tad," she said, delighted.

"He *is* a bit like Tad," Gran agreed. "He's a kind, gentle little boy, and you should stop ordering him around."

"Yeah," said Roy from under his brim. "Stop ordering me around."

Margaret gave his hat a light, happy tap. "What do you have in there for me?" she asked Gran.

"Ta-da!" Gran swept a hanger draped in black plastic out of the closet and swirled it in front of Margaret. "I've been saving this for you, lovey. Not everyone could get away with it, but you can. With your dark hair and eyes, you'll be stunning."

It was Tad's red silk smoking jacket with blue silk lining and butterflies embossed all over it. When Margaret was little, Tad had let her wear it around the house with a pair of Gran's high heels. They used to tie the jacket around her waist with a scarf so she wouldn't trip. Now it came down only to her ankles.

Margaret gathered the silk up around her waist with her hands and turned slowly in front of the full-length mirror at the far end of the closet. "I'll wear it with my green tights, and maybe that velvet cord from your old curtains that's in my bedroom, Gran." She was thrilled by how pretty she looked. She frowned to keep the pleased smile she felt inside from taking over her face, but the smile won out.

Stunning, Gran had said.

"Don't go getting a swelled head, Margaret," said Gran in a teasing voice, watching her. Then, in her usual firm voice, "Pretty is as pretty does."

Gran hung the empty hanger back in the closet and shut the door. "Now, we had better start preparing the food for this party, or I won't have time to get the front door painted."

"The front door?" Margaret and Roy said at the same time.

"Aren't they all supposed to be black?" said Roy.

"They are. But I'm tired of black. Are you with me or agin' me?"

Margaret and Roy looked at each other in silence. Then Margaret gave a resigned shrug. "I guess we're with you, right, Roy?"

"Right."

"Then let's get going," said Gran. "We've got work to do."

Chapter 10.

Mrs. Nightingale wasn't terrible. She was worse than terrible.

She was horrendous. No matter how hard Margaret and Roy clapped, they couldn't cover up the fact that while the music was going in one direction, Mrs. Nightingale's voice was going in the other.

But it didn't matter. The audience loved her. With the long tables pushed against the wall, they were lined up in ragged rows, packing the house. There were people in wheelchairs and people leaning on walkers mixed in with the rest of the crowd. The level of conversation was so loud, it was hard to hear. Then Mrs. Nightingale stood up on the stage with a microphone in one hand and her body swaying back and forth to the music, and they couldn't get enough of her.

They loved her bright green caftan with her matching head scarf and eyelids. They loved the way her little plump feet were stuffed into her narrow green shoes so that it looked as if they would explode like a trick snake out of a can when she took the shoes off.

And they loved her smile. It was bright enough to light up the entire room. Which was fortunate, because the strobe light kept shorting out and plunging the stage into darkness.

Nothing stopped Mrs. Nightingale. She sang one song, then another, then another. Every time a song ended, the audience begged her for more. When she finished the fifth number, she told them she simply had to rest or she was going to fall over dead right here and now, and they'd all have to deal with it. She got down off the stage and came bustling over to Margaret and Roy where they were sitting with Gran. When they stood up to greet her, she smothered them both in a hug that smelled of bay rum.

"I did it!" she said. Her forehead was covered with small beads of sweat, and her lipstick was starting to travel down the fine lines around her mouth. But she was radiant. "I couldn't have done it without you two," she said. "Margaret, you look dazzling. You, too, Roy."

Roy hooked his thumbs in the pink suspenders with the yellow palm trees he had chosen from the box, and grinned.

"Mrs. Nightingale, this is our grandmother," said Margaret. "Elizabeth Mack."

She felt as if she was going to burst, watching them. With pride, because Mrs. Nightingale was so brave, and with love, because Gran, with her beautiful white hair smoothed back into a bun and a blue dress bringing out the startling blue of her eyes, looked so much like her old self again.

"I haven't heard 'Don't Sit Under the Apple Tree' since my husband and I were dating," Gran was saying as they shook hands. "You were wonderful."

"I wasn't," said Mrs. Nightingale. "I was terrible. But let's face it." She leaned toward Gran conspiratorially. "Most of us are deaf by now, anyway."

She slapped her hand to her chest and laughed with such delight, Gran had to join her. Margaret and Roy stood by watching, proud as mother hens.

"You're a very lucky woman, having grandchildren like these," Mrs. Nightingale said at last. "You'll have to let me know the next time they're coming. I'll call my son and tell him to bring Henry. I think you two will like Henry. He's right between you in age."

"Am I mistaken, or has your front door changed color, Mrs. Mack?"

It was Mr. Whiting, resplendent in a blue blazer and polka-dot bow tie. He gave a courtly little bow. "How do you do? I'm Roland Whiting."

"How do you do, Mr. Whiting," Gran said pleasantly. She raised her chin defiantly. "How do you like it?"

"I think it's magnificent, although I'm not sure what the rest of the Steering Committee is going to say."

"I think it's wonderful, Roland." Mrs. Tudley came up to them and slipped her arm through Roy's. "I don't care what the Steering Committee says. It did my heart good, seeing Mrs. Mack's door this afternoon. I think we should all paint our doors different colors. We could make a poster, like the one they have of the doors of Dublin, Ireland." She beamed around the circle at them all. "We could call it The Doors of Carol Woods."

"We might even sell it for our fundraiser for the community garden," said Mr. Whiting. "We still need money for a water line."

"A community garden?" said Gran. There were red spots on both her cheeks.

"Roland has been fighting for one for more than a year," said Mrs. Nightingale. "You wouldn't believe what he's up against. He's had a lot of opposition, but I do think he's worn them down."

"There's an empty lot on Jasmine Street," Mr. Whiting told Gran. "We want to turn it into a garden where any resident who is interested can have a space and share water." He looked wistful. "I haven't been able to grow my Jerusalem artichokes since I moved here."

"I have an old rototiller I'd be happy to share," said Gran. "Perhaps we could build a small shed to store things in so everyone could use them."

"Tubby wore a hat just like that," said Mrs. Tudley, patting Roy's arm. She held her hand out to Gran. "I'm Nelly Tudley, Mrs. Mack. It's a pleasure to meet you."

"It's a pleasure to meet you, too," said Gran. "You made quite an impression on my grandchildren."

It was like watching a play, Margaret thought contentedly. Everyone was saying the right things. Everyone was being polite.

Dominoes, she thought suddenly, falling into place.

"You must be thirsty, Mrs. Nightingale." Gran took control in her reassuring, brisk way. "Why don't we all go back to my house for that party?" She put her arm around Margaret's shoulders. "Mr. Whiting? I believe you're going to join us?"

"Why, thank you, Mrs. Mack. I might stop by my house and collect my accordion, if it's all right with you. Maybe Agatha will favor us with another song. Agatha?" He held out his elbow. "Has anyone ever told you, you sing like a nightingale?"

"Oh, all the time, Mr. Whiting," she said, winking at Margaret and Roy. "All the time."

• • •

The party was a huge success. By the time the guests left, Roy was half-asleep on the couch. Margaret followed Gran into the kitchen with a dirty glass in each hand. "I think Mr. Whiting has a crush on Mrs. Nightingale, don't you?"

"I don't see why not," said Gran. "It's a good thing she stopped him, though. He would have played all night. Put those in the dishwasher, Margaret. We'll worry about the rest in the morning."

"Is anybody home?"

"Dad!" Margaret didn't even think about it. She ran to the front door, threw her arms around his waist, and pressed her face into his chest. She squeezed her eyes shut against a rush of sudden tears. She had never been more glad to see anyone.

"Who have we here?" he said, holding her away from him to get a good look. "This glamorous lady is my daughter?"

"Oh, Dad." She felt ridiculously pleased. "What are you doing here?"

"I brought you a surprise."

"Margaret, look! My new dress!" Claire leaped out from behind Mr. Mack and twirled so that her dress billowed out around her like the umbrella in a fancy drink. It wasn't pink. It was blue, with yellow flowers.

"I can't believe it," said Margaret. She looked at her father in amazement. "How did you talk her into it?"

"We didn't have to. It passed the twirl test."

Claire stopped spinning and threw her arms around Margaret's waist. "Emily and Sarah got one, too! And so will you, as soon as you come home, because of the baby."

"The baby's here?" said Margaret.

"Oh, Matthew, why didn't you call?" Gran came hurrying out of the kitchen with a dishtowel in her hands. "Is everyone all right? Wendy? The baby?"

"Everyone's fine, Mom. Everyone's great," said Mr. Mack, kissing Gran on the cheek. "I didn't call because Claire wouldn't rest until she could tell Margaret herself. In person. Right, Claire?"

They all looked at Claire.

"It's a boy," she said proudly.

"A boy?" said Margaret.

"Margaret said Wendy only has girls," said Roy. He sat up on the couch and rubbed his eyes.

"Not anymore," said Mr. Mack. "This time, she had a nine-pound two-ounce boy."

"I have a brother," Margaret said. It seemed amazing. It seemed impossible. Her heart gave a tiny lurch, like growing pains.

"Oh, Matt, how wonderful," said Gran. She sat down suddenly, her eyes bright. "What does he look like?"

"You mean, *who* does he look like." Mr. Mack rested his hand on Margaret's head. "He looks exactly the way Margaret did when she was born. Do you remember, Mom? She looked like a boxing glove in a black wig."

"The poor little thing," said Margaret. She felt fierce, like a mother lion. "Don't you dare make fun of him."

"What's his name?" said Roy.

"He doesn't have one!" shouted Claire, jumping up and down.

"Why not, Matt?" Gran said.

Her Dad turned to look at her. "Wendy and I think Margaret should be the one to name him. After all, she's the oldest."

"Me?" said Margaret, stunned.

It felt like the most important job she had ever been given. What did *she* know about naming a baby? She'd never had one before. And a boy? Who looked like her? She could feel Gran and her dad watching her.

Well, for one thing, he was going to hate his hair. She knew that. And no matter how much she tried to protect him, Emily and Sarah were going to want to dress him up in doll's clothes all the time, and Claire was going to be after him to play horses with her. . . .

"Tad." She looked at her father with conviction. "His real name can be David, but we'll call him Tad."

For a second she was afraid *his* eyes were bright with tears. But then he grabbed her and held her against him so tightly, she could hardly breathe. "That's my girl," he said into her hair. "Mom? Is that okay with you?"

"It's wonderful," said Gran. "Your father would be so pleased."

Claire started to twirl around the room again. "Now Emily has Sarah, and I have Margaret, and we all have Tad," she sang. "Emily has Sarah, I have Margaret, and we all have Tad."

"And Roy, you can have all of us, anytime you want," said Mr. Mack.

"Tad sure is going to need another boy around," said Roy.

"I'd better tell Wendy so she can stop calling him Baby Mack," said Mr. Mack.

"Let me," said Margaret. "I want to be the one."

"Matthew, you come and open the champagne,"

said Gran. She held out her hand. "And Claire, you and Roy can help me make the Shirley Temples."

Margaret could hear Claire's excited voice in the kitchen as she listened to the phone ringing at the other end. Then she heard Wendy's clear voice. "Hello?"

"Hi, Wendy, it's me. Margaret."

"I know who it is, silly," Wendy said. "How are you?"

"I'm good." Margaret didn't know why, but she suddenly felt shy.

"Did Dad tell you?" said Wendy. "Isn't it wonderful?"

"Yes. Do you want to know what his name is?"

"What?"

"Tad. Well, David, really. But we're going to call him Tad."

"Tad," said Wendy. There was a catch in her voice. "Gran must be very happy."

"Oh, no, don't *you* start crying."

Wendy laughed shakily. "Why, has Gran been upset?"

"She was, but she's okay now. I'll tell you about it when I get home."

"When are you coming? We've missed you. Claire has been beside herself." Margaret heard Wendy's voice change. "Oh. Speaking of Claire."

"What?"

"Your dad and I talked about it after you left," said Wendy. "He was very upset with me about the way I handled the whole business of her sharing your room. And he was right. Not only should I have talked to *him* about it first, but I should have talked to you. I'm sorry."

"That's okay, I don't mind," Margaret said quickly, and was amazed to find that it was true.

"No, it's not okay. But don't worry. Dad's already fixing up the small room off the dining room for Claire. It'll be perfectly fine until we can add on."

"You can't do that," Margaret said. She was appalled. Claire downstairs, by herself? Listening to the sounds of life from upstairs while she lay in the dark alone?

"You can't do that," she said again. "She'll be lonely."

Wendy laughed. "Can you imagine being lonely in a family as noisy as ours?"

"If Claire moves downstairs, I move downstairs," said Margaret firmly. "I want her to stay."

"Are you sure?"

"I'm sure."

"Oh, Margaret, you're so good. When are you coming home?"

• • •

It's a good thing I know how to handle weepy people, Margaret thought as she walked into the kitchen. Wendy was getting to be as bad as Gran.

"Wendy wants us home, first thing in the morning," she announced. "She wants us to bring Gran and Roy, too."

"Here." Her dad handed her a glass. "We were waiting for you to give a toast."

They all raised their glasses. "To Tad, the newest member of the Mack family," said Mr. Mack. "May he be tough enough to survive with four older sisters, poor tyke."

"You can say that again," said Roy.

Claire was spinning around the room, knocking against their chairs. The baby, the dress, seeing Margaret again—it was too much for a six-year-old to take sitting down. The next step beyond elation would be tears.

"Claire, come sit down," said Margaret in a bossy, older sister voice. Claire dutifully climbed into her lap and snuggled down against her. Margaret rested her chin on the top of Claire's head and closed her eyes.

They'd be like bookends, she and Tad. The way Tad and Gran had been for her. A Mack on either end, with the three little girls in between.

Gran was laughing in the background now. Margaret could hear her telling Dad about her plans for her plot in the community garden.

It's a good thing Gran is making so many plans, Margaret thought, yawning contentedly. She'll have to take care of herself a lot more from now on. I'm going to have my hands full.